Having Ca...
distraction

Lauren could tell their physical closeness had a strong effect on him, too. Part of her wanted to back away, to make things easier on him, and another part of her—the part that hadn't had a lover in too long, the part that remembered what an incredible lover Carson was—wanted to pull him against her and kiss him.

She desperately wanted to reach out and touch the light stubble along his jaw. She couldn't help imagining what it would feel like against her face, her breasts, her belly....

The aching between her legs was getting to be too much, and she shifted in her seat.

"You have had a vision about yourself, haven't you?" Carson said.

Lauren smiled. "What I'm having a vision of right now is you and me on that bed, naked. Think you can accommodate me?"

"Are you trying to bewitch me to distract me?"

"Call me wicked," she said. "I won't deny it."

Blaze™

Dear Reader,

I've loved witches ever since I first read Anne Rice's Mayfair witch novels as a teenager. There's just something about powerful women with a hint of supernatural mystique that captures my imagination. Stir in elements of the dark, sensual and forbidden, and my romantic mind runs wild.

I hope you enjoy my take on witch lore in *Call Me Wicked*—a world where tattoos can come alive, anyone could be a witch, or conversely, a member of a secret witch-hunting society. Best of all, it's a place that is unknowingly on the verge of a supernatural revolution.

You can find out more about me and my upcoming books at www.jamiesobrato.com. There you can also e-mail me or participate in my often-gratuitous blog discussions. I'd love to hear from you!

Sincerely,

Jamie Sobrato

CALL ME WICKED
Jamie Sobrato

HARLEQUIN®

TORONTO • NEW YORK • LONDON
AMSTERDAM • PARIS • SYDNEY • HAMBURG
STOCKHOLM • ATHENS • TOKYO • MILAN • MADRID
PRAGUE • WARSAW • BUDAPEST • AUCKLAND

ISBN-13: 978-0-373-79332-7
ISBN-10:   0-373-79332-4

CALL ME WICKED

www.eHarlequin.com

Printed in U.S.A.

ABOUT THE AUTHOR

Jamie Sobrato writes for Harlequin Blaze and lives in Northern California. She is not a witch. She does, however, long for a few supernatural powers, such as the ability to make mean people disappear, and/or the power to turn wheat bread into chocolate. Until she hones those skills, she is content to write about the supernatural in fiction.

To Annelise Robey, the coolest agent
in the known universe

Prologue

"SHE IS ALMOST MORTAL."

Beneath the table, the little girl's ears perked up. The elders were talking about her again. They always forgot she was there.

"It's true, Lauren is the weakest of us all. In another generation, there may be no more witches," her mother said, her voice sounding strange. Not sad, as she should have sounded, but kind of flat and bored, like when she said there was no more honey for the tea.

Lauren sat very still at her mother's feet, under the ebony dining table with its clawed feet and carved legs, and she practiced being invisible. It was her favorite thing to do when the elders were around, and they were so easy to fool with all the big important business they were always busy doing—talking about the quality of grapes or the export of the wine or the upcoming harvest.

"If it weren't for the other child, this generation might have been spared. They are all weakened in their powers, nearly indistinguishable from mortals."

The girl tried not to smile. She had the gift, whether the elders knew it or not. She was just as much a witch as any of them, but she knew how to hide it. She knew how much they disapproved of the children practicing their gifts, so she and her siblings and cousins did it in secret. They snuck out into the vineyards or into the hills to see who was the most powerful, who had learned to move a rock with their mind or make the rain fall hard from the sky. And they had agreed never to tell.

Lauren could sometimes see in her mind things that hadn't happened yet. Prescience, she had once heard her mother call it, because her mother had the same gift, though like the rest of the elders she had sworn never to use it on purpose. Her mother tried not to be powerful.

The grown-ups were not talking about Lauren anymore. Now they were talking about the grapes again, and she didn't care about the grapes, so she closed her eyes and tried to see something that had not happened yet.

It didn't take long. First came a burst of white light behind her eyes, and then came the pictures so clear she felt as if she was living them. She could see a man with brown hair and a woman with long black hair. The woman felt very familiar to her. They were scared; she could feel it. They were running from someone or something. There was sand and darkness and cold wind and the sound of the ocean. A gunshot rang out, and the woman fell to the ground.

In a flash the scene was gone again.

Lauren was shaking. She covered her mouth to keep from crying out and being discovered. She had never seen a person shot before, had never had a vision so scary. She did not know what it meant, but she hoped the woman who was shot would be okay.

Her heart continued to race long after the vision had passed. She willed the shaking to stop, and again sat still, hoping the fear the images evoked would go away, and after a while, it did.

Lauren would not let her gift die the way the elders wanted. She wouldn't live hidden away and afraid all her life. Not when they had her little sister, the most powerful witch ever born, living amongst them, playing with them, reminding them of what they might be if they used their gifts instead of hiding them away.

And when they were grown, there would be a time when witches would never have to hide again. Lauren had seen it happen in her mind.

1

LAUREN PARISH DID NOT intend to die today.

Death was nowhere on her to-do list, and yet here she was, crouched on the fire escape outside her bedroom window, cold wind snaking up her nightgown and her heart pounding wildly in her ears. Four stories up, with two men in black tearing through her apartment and muttering Czech words she could not identify, death didn't seem such an unlikely scenario all of a sudden.

Five minutes ago, she'd been sitting in bed flipping through research notes for a presentation due next week, when an image had flashed in her mind. She saw two men standing at her door, using some kind of tool to pick the lock. When her hearing, more acute than that of mortals, caught the slightest sound of metal against metal at her front door, she'd turned off her bedside lamp, dropped the notes, and scrambled to the window, her only escape. She was easing the window shut again when she heard the men enter the apartment.

It hadn't been the first time one of her visions

had proven useful, but it had definitely been the most opportune.

She barely had enough room to keep herself out of sight of the window on the small landing, and she had to either go up or down. Her breath was coming out in quick shallow gasps, and her legs quaked beneath her. She wanted to cry, but she wouldn't. She had to summon whatever strength she possessed to stay calm, to escape.

She knew without thinking twice who the men were, and she knew their intent without a doubt was to kill her, or take her to be interrogated and then kill her.

Neither choice was remotely appealing.

So this is what it felt like to stare death in the face. It was a fear she hadn't been struck by since childhood, a fear her ancestors had held close and nurtured, a fear she'd foolishly let slip away in her comfortable life—in her disdain for what had always seemed to her generation as the elders' cowardice.

The men only had to feel the still-warm bed where she'd been sitting to know that she'd been there, that she was hiding somewhere close by. She glanced up and saw that her crazy upstairs neighbor was home, but the woman would call the police before she'd let Lauren climb in her window.

She looked down and could see no light coming from the window directly below. The apartment was occupied by a young couple who had a cat they let go in and out the window, and if she was lucky, the window would be open now.

Ever so slowly, she peered into her bedroom again and caught sight of one of the men standing beside her bed, doing exactly what she feared he'd do. Her heart flip-flopped. When he ran his hand along the sheet where she'd been sitting, she held her breath and eased herself slowly toward the ladder.

The old metal fire escape was creaky, and even a cat scaling it had a tendency to sound like a herd of buffalo. Lauren didn't have a chance. Why couldn't she have been born with some really cool power like the ability to shape-shift? Now would have been a great time to transform into a mouse.

She moved as quickly as she could, eased herself down the ladder with a minimum of noise, and stopped at the neighbor's landing. The window, as she suspected, was ajar six inches. But when she tried to push it up farther, she saw that a piece of wood had been nailed into place to prevent the window from opening any wider.

Lauren muttered a curse and glanced up. From above, she could hear her own window opening. She sucked icy air into her lungs and shivered, then pushed up hard on the window. It wouldn't budge. She noticed the wood window frame was rotting, and she had to decide whether to keep trying to get into this window or take the risk of going another floor down.

Above, if they were looking down at her now, they'd see her. She felt a burst of adrenaline, and she stood up, kicked the window frame with all the strength she could summon, and felt the satisfying give of the wood against her heel. Broken glass pierced the top of her foot, but she didn't feel pain, just the warmth of blood.

The men upstairs had to have heard. She broke away a few large shards of remaining glass and eased herself quickly through the opening, where she thankfully found an empty bedroom. She ran to the front door, flung it open, and kept running.

Downstairs, out the door, into the street, through the alley, toward the apartment three blocks over where she could only pray her best friend was home.

Her nightgown didn't protect her from the cold October air, and the cut on her foot was beginning to throb with pain, but she ran, faster than she'd ever run before, her bare feet slapping cold pavement— across streets and around cars and past buildings and up stairs until she was pounding on Macy's door.

When the door opened a moment later, she saw her friend's worried face, and she collapsed into her, into the apartment, then she spun and slammed the door shut. Locked all the locks. Caught her breath.

No one had followed her closely enough to see where she'd gone, she was pretty sure of it. But only now did she feel the weight of guilt that she had possibly led those murderers right to Macy's door.

"Lauren! What happened? What's wrong? Are you okay?" Macy was holding her at arm's length now, taking in her half-naked appearance, her bare feet, the bloody gash.

Lauren heaved a few deep breaths, but said nothing. Macy didn't know Lauren's true identity. No mortal knew.

"Oh my God, your foot! Let me get something," Macy said, hurrying to the bathroom. "Should I call 9-1-1?" she called over her shoulder.

"No!" Lauren eased onto the floor, leaned against the door, fearful now of not being near enough to an exit should she need one.

This was not the first time Lauren had been forced to hide from assholes who had a thing against witches. Once when she was a kid visiting her extended family in Brittany on the coast of France, the house had been raided by the witch hunters, and she'd been forced to hide in the forest for days with her cousins.

She'd grown up in hiding, and she'd been lectured a thousand times about the dangers of being a witch in a world of mortals. But all things drift toward complacency, and even the gravest dangers cannot loom large in one's mind for long when at a distance. There had not been many raids in California during her lifetime—certainly not enough for her to worry about. The Parish family—they'd changed their names from Beauville to Parish when her grandparents had moved from Louisiana to the Napa Valley in the thirties—had been very good at hiding.

So what had changed? Why her? Why now?

She didn't have to consider the questions for more than a second. The CNN interview had done it. It had aired for the first time early this morning. The witch hunters apparently worked fast.

Her mother had been furious, had called her on her cell phone that afternoon to tell her she was a fool and a traitor, had told her she'd put the entire family in danger for the sake of her own ego.

But Lauren hadn't believed her. She'd grown so complacent and secure, smug even. She hadn't seen any harm in doing the interview to talk about the study she'd headed up, the results of which were making news all over the world now. She'd believed the witch hunters weren't really a threat anymore, that most of the zealots among them had died out and that any remaining ones weren't really interested in a battle that was centuries old.

Lauren had been wrong. Her inconsistent and troublesome ability to foretell the future had not warned her far enough in advance. Instead, it had waited until danger was at her door.

Macy returned carrying a towel and a first aid kit. She knelt on the oak plank floor beside Lauren's foot and began tending to the wound. "Is this glass?" she said, gently picking it out as Lauren winced in pain.

"Yeah," she said, looking at her friend instead of the cut. "I had a little accident. I can't really tell you what happened, okay? Can you just trust me and promise not to say a word to anyone about this?"

Macy peered at her with concerned brown eyes. She looked so safe, so surreal here in her warm, familiar apartment, her long blond hair still wet from a shower. "You're scaring me, Lauren. What the hell's going on?"

"I have to disappear for a while, okay? And you can't tell anyone you saw me tonight. You can't act like you know anything at all."

"About what? What are you talking about? Is someone trying to hurt you?"

"I just need you to loan me some clothes, and maybe your car if you can spare it. And some money, just enough to get me away from here."

Lauren's mind raced now, forming a plan. She'd always known what she had to do if she was ever found out. But the logistics of getting to her cousin Sebastian in L.A.—how to get clothes and money when she was chased out of her apartment wearing nothing but a nightgown—were never discussed by the elders.

"God, Lauren, this is crazy. You know you can tell me anything, right? You can trust me."

Macy was wrapping her foot in a bandage now, securing it with tape.

"It's not that simple. And I swear I would tell you if I could. Just trust me on this. As soon as I can, I'll give you the whole story, and this will all make perfect sense, and you'll understand why I'm protecting you by not saying anything."

Macy regarded her seriously. "What about Griffin? Should I not tell him you've been here either?" Griffin was Macy's fiancé.

Lauren shook her head. "Don't tell anyone."

"I think you need stitches in your foot. Can I at least give you a ride to the emergency room?"

She looked down at the bandage. "No. I'll have to have it looked at somewhere else, not here in the city."

Her friend sighed heavily. "Okay, I'll give you whatever you need. You can have my car. I'll just tell Griffin I had to put it in the shop for repair."

"Thank you so much, Macy. You're saving my life right now. And whatever you do, don't go to my apartment. In fact, don't even let on that you know me if anyone asks."

"This is just too weird," Macy said as Lauren followed her into the bedroom. "You're acting like a criminal or something."

It's way worse than that, Lauren wanted to say, but didn't. "Don't worry, I'm not, I swear. When I'm able to explain, you'll understand."

Macy wouldn't have believed the truth anyway. What mortal could without some kind of solid proof? They needed to see milk being curdled on the spot or corpses raised from the dead to believe a witch was in their midst. Not that real witches did any of that stuff, but stereotypes died hard.

Lauren's foot throbbed now, yet she could walk on it with little trouble. Wearing shoes might be a different story, though.

But she had to get out of San Francisco, and she had to do it fast. She wasn't sure if she'd ever be able to come back. At that thought, tears stung her eyes, and when Macy glanced back and caught the stricken look on her face, she halted in her tracks in the doorway to the bedroom.

"Lauren," she said, and took her friend into her arms.

Lauren awkwardly allowed Macy to hug her. She'd never been much for the whole cheek kissing and hugging friends thing. But slowly the gesture comforted her enough to relax into the embrace.

She wasn't the one who broke into tears about anything, ever. She was the scientist, the medical researcher who viewed everything through the cool, impartial lens of science. She was the icy intellectual, the one people relied upon for the harsh, unvarnished truth. While her gift of prescience may have been unpredictable, she'd always relied on her intelligence to solve any problem. She didn't do *this*.

Not cowering. Not weakness. Not falling apart.

She didn't realize right away that she was crying hard, that sobs racked her chest, until she heard Macy murmuring soothing sounds.

And then Lauren stopped. She calmed down, silenced herself, pulled away, wiped her face.

Macy stared at her with concern. "Are you sure you'll be okay to drive? Do you need me to give you a ride somewhere? I'll take you wherever you need to go. I'll drive you all the way to Mexico if—"

Lauren was shaking her head before Macy even stopped speaking. "No, it's not safe for you. I have to go alone."

She nodded. And after a pause she said, "Okay, let's get you packed then."

"You're not expecting Griffin to stop by any time soon, are you?"

"Not too soon—he's hanging out with Carson tonight actually."

"Oh." Carson. Great.

Carson McCullen, Lauren's most recent mortal lover, was a man she had been trying to avoid at all costs for the past two months.

It wasn't easy to take a mortal as a lover. For one thing, it was a practice strictly forbidden by the elders. Not that forbidding anything ever stopped the witches of Lauren's generation from doing whatever the hell they wanted, but this particular forbidden act had its unique complications.

Mortals, with all their weaknesses and sexual limitations, tended to get, well...addicted, when they had sex with a witch. Witches were so much more sensual creatures, so sexually superior, that having sex with one tended to ruin the average mortal for all future encounters of the nonsupernatural variety. And so while Lauren tried her best not to do mortal men, occasionally her appetites got the best of her.

It wasn't easy limiting herself to sex with other witches. For one thing, she was related in some distant or not so distant way to most of the ones she knew—urk!—and for another, witches were forbidden from congregating together in public, so every interaction had to be on the down-low, which got to be a drag real fast.

She tried to be good, and she often traveled abroad to find lovers, but occasionally she grew weak and took a mortal.

Carson was one of those instances.

And entertaining him for that weekend in Vegas had been a favor to Macy, too. She couldn't very well have turned down helping her best friend, not when she was horny as hell and in need of a weekend getaway to boot. So she'd spent one blissful weekend rocking Carson's world, and ever since, he'd been trying to track her down.

To his credit, he'd been an unusually talented mortal lover. She'd never met anyone before who'd satisfied her so thoroughly. But she knew the only way to cure his addiction now was to stay as far away from him as she could. It was the kindest thing to do.

She watched Macy filling an overnight bag with clothes for her, and she glanced at the clock. It was half past eight. She could be in L.A. before morning.

Far away from Carson, which was good, but also far away from her job, her friends, her entire life. Far away from everything she held dear.

But the fear that lurked in her belly told her she had no choice. She had to run as fast as she could, and she had to do it tonight.

2

"HEY, ISN'T THAT LAUREN?"

Carson McCullen nearly spewed his beer across the room when he spotted Lauren Smith's face on the plasma-screen TV. He hadn't seen her in two months, not since the scorching weekend they'd spent together in Las Vegas. And now there she was, being interviewed on CNN Headline News, while he and his best friend, Griffin, gaped at the TV.

"I thought her name was…"

"Lauren Smith," Carson filled in.

But no, her name wasn't Lauren Smith. Right there at the bottom of the screen, the text said her name was Lauren Parish, medical researcher at San Francisco Pacific University.

He blinked as the facts settled themselves in his brain.

That would explain his inability to track down Lauren Smith, who did not work at Western Airlines the way she'd claimed. Aside from one unpleasant phone conversation, they'd had no contact since Las Vegas, in spite of Carson's crazed urges to see her again.

He had never been addicted to a woman before. He'd been infatuated, enthralled, aroused, in love and in lust, but addicted? No.

Then came Lauren, a woman he had not been able to stop thinking about for the past two months, a woman who'd possessed him so thoroughly, he was willing to make a complete ass of himself to have another chance with her.

Some more words came flying at him from the TV. Words like *sex* and *reduced IQ* and *weakened recall skills*. He grabbed the remote and hit the rewind button—thank God for TiVo—then listened all over again as Lauren talked about the study she'd apparently conducted, which proved that sex really was responsible for making people stupid.

Or in her words, *sexual orgasm led to a temporarily reduced intellectual capacity in humans.*

What the hell?

He cast a disbelieving glance at Griffin lounging on the other end of the couch. Griffin, who'd been in Vegas that weekend, and who'd met Lauren "the flight attendant" Smith, as well. In fact Griffin's very own fiancée, Macy, had helped perpetrate the lies about her friend.

"Dude," Griffin said, shaking his head. "I'm as stunned as you are. I had no idea."

The woman on TV, although she looked identical to the Lauren Carson had spent that frenzied weekend making love to, didn't sound much like her. This Lauren was clearly a brainiac, with a vocabulary to rival Webster's and a look that only whispered sexpot. Sure, she was still sexy, but her blatant sensuality was hidden behind an austere black blazer and top, trendy little black-rimmed glasses and a severe bun that tamed her long dark hair and made her look less like a Goth Angelina Jolie and more like the object of someone's kinky dominatrix school mistress fantasy.

When the interview ended, Carson backed up the segment again and watched a third time. "I don't freaking believe this. She's the same woman, right? We're not imagining this, are we?"

Griffin shook his head. "They even said she's right here in San Francisco. I can't believe Macy didn't tell me…."

"Oh hey, don't let this come between you two. You know how women are—she was probably sworn to secrecy or something."

"So are you gonna stop jonesing over this chick and go find her now?"

Carson hesitated, but he knew the answer in his gut without saying a word. Hell yeah. He was going to find her, and he was going to find a way to get another chance with her, whomever she really was.

Lauren Parish, medical researcher at San Francisco Pacific University?

Not at all who she'd led him to believe she was. He wasn't sure whether to be amused or pissed off. Sure, Las Vegas was a town where people lied about their names and behaved in ways they wouldn't in their everyday lives, and with any other woman, Carson would have let it go.

But this woman—she'd gotten to him. She'd worked her way under his skin, and he'd barely been able to function, he craved her so badly. This woman—this woman he'd fantasized about constantly, wasn't the woman he thought he'd been with at all.

He'd tried to imagine her true identity, pictured her sitting in an office somewhere, or even working as a flight attendant for some other airline than the one she'd told him. But he'd never imagined this. He paused the screen with Lauren's image on it. No doubt it was her.

She was a scientist. A scientist who'd discovered sex's dirty little secret, according to CNN.

No wonder she'd lied about her profession. Had she been experimenting on him? Testing him to see how dumb she could make him in one hot weekend? Or had she been as hot for him as he had been for her?

"So do you think she was like, experimenting on me?"

"What do you mean?"

"You know, that weekend, all the, ah, bedroom activities. Do you think she was testing out her hypothesis on me or something?"

Griffin laughed. "I think she'd lose her standing in the scientific community if her research methods involved Vegas hotels and alcoholic beverages."

"I guess," Carson muttered, not feeling very convinced.

"Hey, medical researchers have to get laid, too. I'm sure she was into you."

Carson stood and went to Griffin's desk, opened the Web browser on the computer, and navigated to a directory Web site, then typed in Lauren's correct name and city. A few seconds later, an address he didn't recognize popped up, and he read it aloud to Griffin.

"Hey, that's like three or four blocks from Macy's place."

Carson stared at the address. He could hardly believe he now had a way to see Lauren face-to-face again. This woman who'd wrought wonders on his body and haunted his fantasies was only minutes away.

Why did it matter so much that he try one more time to have a second chance with her? In his gut he knew without a doubt...

She made him feel alive. In his entire wild-child life, he'd tried everything and done everything. He'd begun to fear his picture appeared on UrbanDictionary.com beside the word *jaded.* He'd started to believe there was nothing left in life that would thrill him, nothing that would ever truly excite him again.

There were downsides to growing up a spoiled upper-middle-class brat, having the cushy house in Woodside and the mom who drove the Mercedes wagon, the Brazilian nanny and the Christmases in the Tahoe vacation house with the million-dollar views of the lake. Carson had had it too easy. He knew this about himself, and he knew he'd taken it all for granted.

Whatever he'd gotten in life, he'd gotten by coasting, because he'd always been too busy chasing after the latest thrill or the latest honey to give a damn about anything else.

Until Lauren. Not only did she make him feel alive, but he had a feeling she could make him care about something again, and he wanted to find out if he was right.

"I was being all eco-conscious and took the Muni over here. Do you know if it stops in that neighborhood?"

"Are you for real?" Griffin said. "You're just going to go over there and drop in on her unannounced?"

Was he?

"Yeah," he finally said. "I think we had such a strong physical connection, if she sees me face-to-face, she won't be able to slam the door on me."

"You're going to wait until daylight, though, right? You know, so she doesn't call the police on you and have you arrested for stalking her?"

Carson glanced at his watch. "It's only eight-thirty. Not too late to drop in for a friendly visit."

"If you're determined to make an ass of yourself, I can give you a ride just to witness the spectacle. I'm spending the night at Macy's anyway."

Carson clicked Print on the Web browser, and a few seconds later Griffin's printer spit out Lauren's street address. He folded up the sheet of paper and put it in his pocket.

He was vaguely aware that his behavior had left the realm of normal and entered might-be-mistaken-for-a-lunatic territory, but he was having a hell of a hard time caring about appearances right now. Not when he had a chance to see Lauren again.

"Okay, man, let's go."

Fifteen minutes later, they were parking outside the address. He stared up at the building where Lauren lived and felt a pang of desire hit him like a brick wall. God, how could he want a woman so badly who apparently didn't want him? He wasn't sure he wanted to explore any answers to that question, so he took a deep breath and got out of the car.

Before shutting the door, he leaned down to look at Griffin and said, "I can catch the Muni back home if you don't want to wait."

"I wouldn't miss this for the world. I'm sitting right here."

"What if she invites me in?" Carson said, realizing he sounded a little too pie-in-the-sky hopeful.

Griffin laughed. "Come back out or call me on your cell to tell me to go. Until I get the word from you, I'll be here."

He sat back in his seat and cranked the stereo, and Carson slammed the door.

He climbed the stairs to her apartment two at a time, his heart racing and his mind whirling around the fact that he was about to knock on her door, possibly about to see her again. Finally.

He hadn't even brushed his damn teeth. Pausing at the top of the steps, he dug around in his wallet and found an emergency piece of gum tucked into one of the credit card slots, unwrapped it, and popped it in his mouth. Much better. He couldn't meet the woman of his erotic dreams with dog breath.

But when he arrived at Lauren's door, he found it ajar. He knocked tentatively, waited, then when he heard no sounds coming from within, he stepped inside.

A coatrack lay across the floor at his feet, and all around the wreckage of the apartment suggested something was seriously wrong. Papers, pillows, toppled furniture and the various items of everyday life were strewn about, cluttering the floor. Either Lauren was allergic to housework, or someone had trashed her place.

His chest tightened.

Where was she? He stepped over some books that had been knocked off shelves and went to the bedroom, where a similar state of disarray prevailed. A window gaped open next to the bed, and cold air poured in. Had someone broken into the apartment via the window?

Had Lauren been home? Was she hurt, or worse? His gut clenched at the thought.

No one was in the bathroom, either, nor the kitchen when he peered into it. Something was seriously wrong, and his brain was only starting to catch up to the facts. Careful not to touch anything unnecessarily and damage evidence, he eased Lauren's front door closed, then ran back downstairs to Griffin's car.

Griffin was staring at his PDA when Carson pounded on the driver's side window. He frowned and lowered the window.

"What's wrong?"

"I don't know what the hell's going on, but Lauren's place is trashed, and she's not home."

"You went in?"

"The door was wide-open. I think we need to call the police or something."

"That's crazy. Let me call Macy first and see if she's heard from Lauren." He hit a couple of buttons on the PDA, then held it to his ear.

A few seconds later he was talking to Macy, explaining the situation, then listening, then saying "Oh" and "Uh-huh."

He hung up and stared at Carson again looking as if he'd just received news that Elvis was actually alive and hiding out in the trunk of his car.

"What's going on?"

"I'm not sure, but I think my girl has lost her mind."

"Griffin, what the hell is going on?" Carson demanded with a little more force as his stomach coiled itself into a bigger knot.

"She said we shouldn't call the police, and that we need to get out of here as fast as we can. That we have to make sure we're not followed, before going to a gas station three blocks north of here. Lauren is supposed to meet us there."

Carson looked around, wondering who it was that might follow them. And why the cloak-and-dagger routine? Lauren was going to meet them? Lauren was there with Macy right now? This was all too weird to even wrap his brain around. He felt as if all the key facts were missing, and yet at the same time, his pulse quickened at the thought that Lauren was only a few blocks away, out of his reach…but not for long.

He had to shake himself to remember the fact that she was in some kind of trouble.

He got in the car, then Griffin started driving in the opposite direction and making a few turns to shake off any possible tail before finally heading north. The entire time Carson watched out the rear window to make sure no one was trailing them. As they were pulling into a gas station out of the shadows on the side of the building emerged the woman he'd been aching for months to see.

She was more stunning in real life than he remembered. She had a strange, cool, sexual energy about her that made her seem almost otherworldly. Not like a mere mortal, but like some sex goddess come to Earth to bring to life his every fantasy.

Her long black hair draped her shoulders and

chest, framing a face so ethereally pretty, he had a hard time looking away from it. She was tall—at least five-nine and the only woman he'd ever been with who could look him in the eye when she wore heels—and her body was lean and catlike, with a few lush curves thrown in to make things even more interesting.

She motioned for them to park, then she climbed into the backseat, all the while her gaze only brushing past Carson, barely acknowledging his presence. Her spicy-sweet scent wafted over him and his cock went hard instantly.

"Drive," she said by way of greeting. "Fast."

3

LAUREN HATED HERSELF for getting caught without a plan. She didn't want anyone else involved in the danger she faced now, but already three innocent mortals had been pulled into it.

"Where are we headed?" Griffin asked as he glanced at her in the rearview mirror.

"Macy's going to let me borrow her car, but I wanted to talk to you two first. She's going to meet us at Stonestown Mall."

"Going shopping?"

"Not exactly," Lauren said, not wanting to give away any more information than necessary. "I'm sorry I can't tell you what's going on. I'd really appreciate your not asking me any questions right now."

Carson was sitting sideways, watching her over the back of the passenger seat. He seemed shocked to see her again, and if she hadn't been so damn scared, she might have been able to summon some surprise herself.

"I saw you on the news," he said.

"What were you doing at my apartment?"

Lauren finally remembered her seat belt and buckled herself in as the car turned a corner.

"I wanted to say hi."

"How'd you find me?" she asked, her stomach queasy.

"The magic of the Internet. It was easy once I had your real name from the CNN interview."

Apparently The Order had found it easy, too. Or was she being paranoid? Was it possible the men who'd broken into her apartment had just been run-of-the-mill meth addicts looking for something to steal?

Her brain couldn't dwell on a single thought for long. One thing she'd had hammered into her relentlessly her entire life was that there was no such thing as too much paranoia where The Order was concerned.

"You went to my door and knocked?" she asked Carson.

"Yeah, but the door was open. I looked inside and saw that the place was empty, and then I left. Why?"

"Did you see anyone, or did anyone see you?"

"I don't know."

"Griffin, did you stay in the car or go to my apartment?"

"I stayed in the car."

The witch hunters had been known to leave surveillance equipment behind after they invaded a witch's residence, and they very well could have video footage of Carson now.

"When are you going to tell us what's going on?" Carson asked.

She covered her face with her hands and sighed. This was all too much, too fast. She would have to take Carson with her. He wouldn't be safe in San Francisco.

"Just give me some time to think," she muttered.

Lauren's heartbeat didn't return to normal until they were well out of her neighborhood. That damn study. It had endangered not only her, but her friends, and Carson. How had she been so stupid?

Why hadn't she paid more attention to the elders' warnings?

Lauren had spent most of her adult life too busy working toward her career goals to worry much about clan politics and fear. Her intelligence was stronger than her unpredictable gift of prescience, so she'd gone with her greatest strength, graduating summa cum laude from Stanford with a Master's in human biology, then taking a much-sought-after position at a major university, where she'd gotten involved in sexuality studies.

Her entire adult life, aside from a minor rebellion at the age of eighteen, had been normal and free of danger. It had made her get sloppy.

The guys in the front seat had fallen into an uncomfortable silence, probably trying to decide whether Lauren needed to be hauled to the nearest police precinct or mental hospital, rather than the mall.

Traffic was light, and in fifteen minutes they

made it to the mall parking lot. Lauren had already warned Macy that they had to do a quick exchange of cars and not linger talking.

When they pulled into the lot beside Macy's car, Lauren leaned forward and said, "Carson, I need you to come with me, okay?"

He gave her an odd look, but shrugged and said, "Sure."

"Griffin, Macy's going to get in the car with you. I want you and Macy to leave, be careful to make sure no one's following you, and don't ever go back to my apartment again." She held his gaze until he nodded. "Carson and I will be in contact again as soon as we can, but don't worry if you don't hear from us for a while."

Carson's expression was growing more concerned by the second. "Um, any minute now would be a good time to tell me what the hell's going on."

"You'll have to let someone at your office know that you won't be in for a few days—at the least."

He looked at her as though she'd lost her mind. "Just as soon as you tell me what's going on."

Lauren bit her lip, but said nothing. If she'd been smart, she would have come up with some great cover story to not alarm them all so much.

"Let's get in Macy's car, and then I'll explain."

Carson did as instructed, exiting Griffin's car without any more protest. Good thing he probably would have walked through fire to get some time alone with her.

Outside the car, Lauren gave Macy a quick hug, took the car key she offered, and waved goodbye to Griffin. Once in the car with Carson, they watched as Macy and Griffin drove away.

"We have to find a pay phone. I think there's one on the other side of the mall," she said as she started the car.

"I've got my cell phone—you can use that," Carson said.

"No, it's not secure enough."

"Are you like a spy or something?" he asked.

"I wish it was that simple."

The mall parking lot had emptied out at this time of night, and the remaining cars were clustered around the restaurants that stayed open late. Lauren spotted a pay phone and pulled over near it.

The farther she got from the invasion of her apartment, the less real it felt. She could have almost convinced herself it had only been a bad dream, except for the gash on her foot that was still aching.

She looked over at Carson in the passenger seat and allowed herself to really take in his presence for the first time, now that they were alone together.

His wavy brown hair had grown since she'd last seen him, brushing his collar, and he now sported a five o'clock shadow that hadn't been there in Vegas. He was tall and substantial with his wiry, athletic physique and his broad, rock-hard shoulders.

He wore a black turtleneck, black leather jacket, and a pair of faded jeans that fit him so well they would have driven her to distraction at any other time. A pair of black Doc Marten's completed his look, which was the sort of carefully planned casualness that said he cared about his appearance but didn't want to look as though he was trying too hard.

"So do I get the scoop now?"

"I need to make a phone call or two, and then I'll explain everything as best I can."

In truth, she needed more time to decide how much information she could risk giving him.

He studied her. "Sex makes us dumb, eh?"

"Don't worry," she said. "I wasn't experimenting on you in Vegas. I promise."

"That's reassuring to know, I guess. But it doesn't explain why you've gone to such lengths to avoid me."

Lauren shrugged. "I just wanted a weekend fling. I though you did, too."

"Am I allowed to change my mind?" he asked with a cocky little half smile.

"Is that the real reason you came to my apartment? To interrogate me about why I'm not really a flight attendant named Lauren Smith?"

"I came to visit because I wanted a real explanation. Well, that and a chance to see you again."

Then this was his unlucky day. "You'll probably wish we'd never met by the time I explain everything."

"I'm all ears."

"I'll be right back. Just let me make these calls." She fished some quarters out of Macy's storage compartment and exited the car.

Outside, in the cold night air, she felt exposed and vulnerable. With shaking hands she inserted some quarters and called her mother.

Now her hands shook? Not a half hour ago when she was fighting for her life, but now that she had to face the wrath of her mother…

The phone rang five times before someone picked up. "Parish residence," the maid answered.

"It's Lauren. I need to speak with my mother right now."

"I believe she's retired for the evening."

"Wake her up. It's an emergency."

"One moment please."

Lauren scanned the area, but no one looked suspicious. The patrons of the nearby restaurant were absorbed in their own lives, paying no attention to her. She glanced toward the car and caught Carson's eye. His expression inscrutable, he watched her as she watched him, and she got the feeling he wasn't nearly as calm as he looked. She couldn't blame him.

A moment later her mother's voice came on the line. She had a remarkable ability to never sound as though she'd just woken up. "What is it, Lauren? Bette said it was urgent."

Lauren took a deep breath. "The Order found me. I'm not sure how, but I think it must have had something to do with my TV appearance."

Silence, and then, "How did you get away? Where are you now?"

"That's not important. I need to figure out how exactly they found me."

"I hope you understand now why we should shun the spotlight—"

"This isn't the time for lectures. Of course I understand."

"You know, you bear a remarkable resemblance to your great-grandmother, who was, of course, killed by The Order. Maybe that's how they recognized you."

"But that was over a hundred years ago."

"They don't forget. And I'm sure they keep photos of all known witches on file for occasions like this."

The truth sank in, and Lauren felt her dinner churning in her stomach, threatening to rise up into her throat. She steadied herself against the pay phone, pressed her forehead to the cool metal surface of its frame.

Her stupid moment in the spotlight would lead to her own doom. Now that she'd been ID'd by witch hunters, she'd spend the rest of her goddamn life on the run, fearing death at the hands of The Order, never safe.

"Lauren? Are you there?"

She wasn't sure if she'd missed anything her mother had said. Only now she realized her ears had been filled with a hissing sound that was subsiding as she gained control of herself again.

"I'm here. I didn't realize…I mean, I forgot about my great-grandmother."

"Well, you've made quite a mess of things, haven't you?"

"I'm going to disappear for a while."

"Yes, I imagine so. You'll need to enlist Sebastian's help."

"I'm not sure he will. There's a mortal involved, and I have to protect him, too."

Again, silence filled the line, and then her mother expelled an exasperated sigh.

"Don't tell me you've been consorting with—"

"I'm not going to talk about this right now. I have to go. I just wanted you to know what's happening, why I've disappeared," Lauren blurted, filling the line with words. "I love you, Mom. Bye."

She hung up the phone, knowing she was risking her mother's considerable wrath by doing so. But getting to Sebastian for help was more important than her mother's temper tantrum. He'd been her closest childhood friend, and maybe based on that old allegiance, he might consider helping a mortal, too.

Or not.

Lauren stared at the receiver resting in its cradle as she tried to remember Sebastian's number, which she'd been forbidden to write down. It had been over a year since she'd seen him, many months since they'd spoken on the phone.

Slowly, the numbers came to her. She inserted more coins, then dialed and waited. After a few rings voice mail picked up. His recording sounded in his unmistakably laid-back style. She'd never once seen him get flustered, shaken or perturbed.

He was the epitome of cool, unlike her right now.

"Hi, it's me…" She hesitated, then decided not to say her name as she realized leaving any specific details might be too dangerous. With luck Sebastian would recognize her voice. "I'm coming for a visit, and I'll be there before morning. Don't call my cell phone, though—it's not safe. I'll find you when I get there."

So she had no choice but to go to Sebastian's club in West Hollywood and hope like hell he wouldn't send her and Carson away. Because if he did, she had nowhere else to turn.

She hung up the phone and wondered belatedly if it had been a mistake to leave a message at all. Her paranoia was growing by the second.

She glanced around again, but there were no shadowy figures lurking about, no one staring in her direction. Well, except Carson.

How to tell him? And *what* to tell him?

As a child, she'd occasionally imagined revealing the truth about herself and her family to a mortal. She'd imagined their reaction, their awe at the powers she possessed, and she'd gotten a thrill from it. But that was before she'd been old enough to fully understand the inherent dangers of the truth.

Lauren hurried back to the passenger door since Carson had switched to the driver's seat and got in. He studied her.

"Well?" he said.

She had no idea how to tell him. She took a deep breath and said, "What I have to say you probably won't believe. But it's really important that you believe it anyway."

He drummed his fingers on the steering wheel, as if doing so was a response in itself.

"Okay, so what is it?" he finally asked.

"Another thing—I need to know that you're trustworthy. If I tell you this thing, it's a secret you'll have to keep your whole life. You can't ever tell anyone. If you do, lots of people could die, including you."

His expression was growing more alarmed by the second. "You can trust me."

Based on Macy's and Griffin's adoration of Carson, she was almost sure she could take his word for that.

"Just so you know, I don't have any choice but to trust you. And you don't have any choice but to keep this secret. Since you might have been spotted in my apartment, the people who are after me are going to want to kill you, too."

He looked outraged. "Who's trying to kill you? What kind of trouble are you in? Lauren, please tell me what the hell's going on."

"Just slow down. It's going to take a while to explain everything."

He expelled a ragged breath. "I've got all night."

The words had never crossed her lips before, and saying them aloud was an act so foreign, she almost couldn't do it. She looked Carson in the eyes, swallowed her fear, and said it.

"I'm a witch."

CARSON HAD OFFICIALLY heard it all now, and he would have laughed except Lauren looked dead serious.

A witch? "Is that a PC way of saying *bitch,* or do you mean you're like one of those goth people who goes around trying to cast spells and stuff."

"Neither," she said.

And he listened as she explained. As she talked, he drove south toward the highway, and before she'd finished explaining, they were passing through San Jose.

Carson half believed her and half suspected she was suffering from an undiagnosed case of schizophrenia. He asked questions here and there, but mostly he listened in amazement to her elaborate tale of ancient witch clans and secret orders of witch hunters and genetic differences between witches and humans, and how she didn't cast spells but she did have some kind of supernatural power.

By the time she was done, they were several hours south of San Francisco, well on their way toward the underground safe house Lauren claimed they were headed to in West Hollywood, and Carson's head was spinning.

"I know this all sounds crazy, and you probably don't believe me," she said. "But I appreciate your trying to understand."

"I admit I'm a little suspicious about your sanity," he said.

"Do you remember how awful you felt after you left Las Vegas? Probably like you were coming down off a high and going through withdrawal symptoms?"

"Yeah, how'd you know?"

"That's what happens to mortals who have sex with witches. You get addicted. That's why you couldn't leave me alone and couldn't stop thinking about trying to get in touch with me again."

"Addicted?"

Lauren nodded. "Not to brag, but mortals tend to find sex with a witch by far the best sex of their lives, and the chemicals released during orgasm are so intense they create an addiction."

That certainly explained a lot.

"So, let's say I tentatively believe you. How long will I have to stay at this place in L.A.?"

Lauren stared at him, looking grim. "I don't know," she said. "It depends on what my cousin says when we get there. He's the expert on evading the witch hunters."

"Is it okay if I use my cell phone now to leave a message at work that I won't be in for a while?"

"Yes," she said. "Go ahead. Just say you've had a family emergency. But don't leave any information about where you are or where you're going."

Carson did as instructed. There was a big meeting he'd miss tomorrow, and someone would have to fill in for him there. Not to mention the rest of his jam-packed schedule for the week. But as he explained the situation to his boss's voice mail box, he felt a sense of excitement filling his chest.

Why the hell would he care about missing some boring-ass meetings with ad agency clients when he could be running off to L.A. with the woman of his fantasies?

And, he realized, he actually wanted to believe Lauren's story. It had everything his life was lacking—danger, intrigue, mind-blowing sex….

Carson had always felt like a trapped animal in his buttoned-up workaday life, and now, for the first time he could remember, he was feeling as though someone had finally opened up the cage and set him free.

4

SOMEWHERE ALONG I-5, they stopped at a rest area and traded seats so that Lauren could drive. Carson finally must have given in to exhaustion and fallen asleep, he realized as he woke up at a stop light. He'd asked for Lauren to let him drive again whenever she got tired herself, but she insisted she was so hyped up on adrenaline there was no way she could sleep, and she wanted him to rest if he could.

"Where are we?" he asked as he stretched and yawned.

Outside, it was still dark.

"We're almost there," she said. "My cousin operates a network of safe houses for witches in trouble, and his center of operation is on the edge of West Hollywood. He runs a nightclub located in the lobby of a hotel. Hopefully he'll have room for us at the hotel."

Lauren turned into a parking garage, parked the car then turned to him. "My cousin Sebastian may be hostile toward you. Just stay calm and take my lead, okay?"

"Should I be packing a weapon or something?"

"No, but try not to let him get to you. He's like my brother, and aside from the fact that he dislikes mortals, he won't be thrilled with the relationship I've had with you."

"I promise I'll stay cool," he said.

They got out of the car and took an elevator up to a darkened nightclub that was still busy even at what must have been past the legal closing time.

Carson followed Lauren along a dim corridor lit by eerie red lights. They passed one person after another who stared at him as if he were the most un-welcome person they'd ever encountered. He was beginning to get a complex.

"Friendly bunch," he muttered to himself, but Lauren overheard.

"They consider this a mortal-free zone. They can sense you're not one of us."

"Should I get a pointy black hat and a broom?"

Lauren ignored his bad joke and led him into an open area in the noisy nightclub, where the deafen-ing bass of house music set the beat for the pulsing crowd of bodies on a large dance floor. Carson took in the industrial-goes-Goth decor, and the great mass of people, and he wanted to get the hell out. Instead, he continued to follow Lauren as she wound through the throng toward the bar that sat on one side of the club.

The bar was full, but she whispered something into the ear of a man sitting at the end, and he grabbed the hand of the woman next to him and they vacated their seats without looking back.

Weird. Had she cast some kind of spell on them? No, she'd said real witches didn't do that kind of stuff.

They sat and the bartender spotted them immediately. A smile transformed his face when he recognized Lauren, but a moment later when his gaze settled on Carson, his expression turned to cold suspicion.

Lauren leaned over and said to Carson, "That's my cousin. Just let me handle him."

Carson didn't have time to respond before the man rounded the corner of the bar and swept Lauren up into a hug. When they parted, he said, "Cousin, it's been too long."

"Yes," she said. "It has." Then she turned her gaze to Carson. "Sebastian, this is my friend Carson. I'm sorry to be blunt. Did you get my voice mail message saying I was coming for a visit?"

"Come to my office," he said, and they were up again and following him beyond the bar, through a door marked Employees Only and down another long dark corridor, its walls painted black, until they reached an unmarked door. Sebastian let them in.

The office was spare and dimly lit, equipped with a desk, a couple of visitors' chairs, a couch and a black wall unit with sleek black doors that Carson imagined hid some interesting secrets.

Sebastian leaned against the edge of the desk and crossed his arms over his chest. For the first time, Carson took him in as more than another tall, hostile witch.

Or since he was a guy, did that mean he was a warlock? Could men be witches?

Sebastian looked a little like Lauren. At least they shared the same stature, bone structure and hair color. His hair was long and pulled back in a ponytail. His eyes were a haunting, inscrutable gray-green, an odd color against his pale skin. It made him appear otherworldly…as he pretty much was.

On his left hand and arm was a disturbingly realistic tattoo of a sleek black raven, and on his right shoulder was the start of an elaborate patterned tattoo that must have covered at least part of his shoulder and ended halfway up his neck.

His gaze, fixed on Carson with open intensity, seemed somehow connected to the piercing eye of the raven on his hand and forearm.

"Sebastian, I know Carson is mortal, but I need you to put that aside and listen to me."

"I don't help mortals," he said evenly, his gaze finally settling on Lauren.

"There's an exception to every rule, right?"

"Tell me why I should make an exception."

Carson listened as Lauren recounted the story of the men who'd shown up in her apartment, her suspicion that The Order had found her because of the CNN interview, Carson's stumbling upon her apartment and her fear that he, too, was now at risk.

"You don't know if the men saw him?"

"No. I can only assume they planted a camera in my apartment and are probably watching it now. We've heard of that happening, right?"

Sebastian nodded. "Yes. You can't go back there."

"I'm worried about my other friends, too. One of them drove Carson to my house. And after fleeing my apartment, I ran to a friend's house—"

"Both humans?"

Lauren nodded, her gaze fixed on the raven tattoo now.

Carson glanced down at it and could have sworn that he saw it move, but when he watched it further, he saw nothing. All this hocus-pocus crap had his mind tripping out.

"Your friends in San Francisco should be fine. And him," he said with a dismissive gesture to Carson, "you should never have brought him here."

"I know he's supposed to help me, Sebastian," Lauren said, then hesitated. "I had a vision."

Carson blinked at this news. Was she telling the truth? Had she really had a vision about him?

Sebastian was glaring at Lauren now. "You are saying too much."

"He knows everything. That's the other reason I need you to help him."

"I don't protect mortals," he said. "You know I don't, and you shouldn't be asking me to."

"I have as much reason as you do to feel that way," she said.

"You're the one consorting with them."

"You're starting to sound like one of the elders," she said in a tone of voice that let Carson know that was just about the worst accusation she could make.

Sebastian glared at them both.

"You were with me in the forest in Bretagne," Lauren said, and then she started speaking urgently in French.

Carson tried to follow the words, but his one year of college French didn't get him anywhere near understanding what she was saying. He watched her face, the cool intensity of it, and he watched Sebastian's expression transform ever-so-slightly from impenetrable to perhaps willing to relent.

The uncaged feeling that had possessed Carson earlier was settling now into a sense of vague uncertainty. He wasn't sure he wanted to glimpse real freedom, only to have it snatched away before he'd had the chance to taste it. Did he want to be confined here to Sebastian's compound? Or was he intoxicated by the idea of being on the run with Lauren, destination unknown?

He was a fool, he realized, if he thought his lame little sense of adventure mattered at all in the face of Lauren's life being in danger.

"One night," Sebastian finally said when she stopped. "I'll find a place for you for one night, and then you have to get him the hell out of here."

But when he looked at Carson again, his expression said something different. His expression was—

and Carson didn't think he was overstating things here—murderous.

Carson found himself in a staring contest with Sebastian now, neither of them willing to blink, neither willing to look away. But then some movement from the man's hand caught Carson's eye again, and when he looked down the raven tattoo was gone.

LAUREN COULDN'T SHAKE the feeling of doom that had settled on her when she'd been arguing with Sebastian. Without his cooperation—and for more than just a night—they were screwed.

She had not been a visitor in her cousin's world since the age of eighteen. She remembered it all, the freedom, the sense of living authentically. But by the end of that rebellious summer when she'd run away from home and toyed with a life of living underground as a real witch—instead of being the repressed, half witch she lived as now—she'd succumbed to Sebastian's advice that she was far too intelligent and talented to not do something important with her life.

Her cousin had only one room left in the building, a bedroom with one bed and a cot he'd had brought up by an attendant with the understanding that Carson would sleep on it. World-weary as Sebastian was, he could be a little old-school about things on occasion.

"You look like you're seeing a ghost," Carson said as he sat down on the edge of the bed.

Lauren snapped out of her survey of the hotel room with its minimalist furnishings and its air of quiet where she'd spent that summer so long ago, hiding out from the world, a temporary rebel.

"I guess I am. A ghost of my own life, anyway. I was here once before."

"This isn't your first time running for your life?"

Lauren shook her head. "That's not why I was here. I was just running away from my overbearing family back then. Fresh out of high school and refusing to go along with their plans for me."

She sat down on the edge of the bed and winced at the throbbing pain in her foot. She didn't want to risk going to a hospital, so she'd either have to have Sebastian sew up the cut, or hope it healed well enough on its own. She was too tired to think about it right now.

But then she thought of the broken window glass, and how she must have left her blood behind on it. The witch hunters could sample her DNA from the blood, and they'd know for sure that she was a witch. But no, they didn't even have to do that, she realized. They'd surely take a hairbrush from her bathroom, and have all the evidence they'd need to kill her stuck in the bristles of her brush.

"Is your foot going to be okay?"

"Yeah, it's nothing." She hoped.

"So…you ran away to Hollywood and…?"

She shrugged, her gut twisting at the thought of a life she hadn't had the balls to live out back then.

"And nothing. I had a head full of stupid ideas, and I eventually realized I should be doing something productive with my life, so I gave in and went to Stanford just like Mother wanted."

"I hate to bring this up now, when your cousin is probably eavesdropping outside our door, but what the hell was with that tattoo on his arm. Did that thing—"

Lauren cut her gaze at him so sharply he went silent. Her heart pounded in her ears.

"Did it what?"

"Nothing. I was probably just seeing things. I'm delirious from exhaustion."

"Tell me what you think you saw," she demanded.

She'd never met a human who could see the movement of a witch's tattoo. She herself had a tattoo that did not move, but it was on the back of her neck, always hidden by her hair unless she chose to show it to someone.

She'd heard of humans who had witch blood, and who could see the supernatural even though they had no special gifts themselves, but it never would have occurred to her that Carson might be one of those humans.

"That raven. I swear it was looking at me. And then it was like it moved or something, and then it was gone."

"Are you sure?"

"I thought you saw it, too. I noticed you looking at it when it moved."

He'd definitely seen what she had. Did this mean he had witch ancestry?

Lauren took his large, perfectly shaped hands into hers. She turned them over so that she could see his palms, both wanting it to be true and yet knowing it would make no difference. Even if he had a bit of witch blood, he was still off-limits to her according to the elders. He was still human.

"You're not about to read my palms, are you?"

"No," she said, studying them intently.

"Then what the hell are you doing?"

"Could you shut up for one minute?"

Carson went silent.

The lines of his palms intersected, like human palms, but two of the major lines did not intersect with any others—one of the marks of witch blood.

"Pure-blooded humans cannot see the supernatural in action," she finally explained when she looked up at him. "You are not pure-blooded."

"What does that mean?"

"One or more of your ancestors was a witch."

His eyebrows shot up. "So I'm still wondering, what the hell does that mean?"

She shrugged. "Not much. You're human, but you might show an occasional witch trait, like the ability to see Sebastian's tattoo move."

Carson's expression rested somewhere between amused and freaked-out. "This is getting weirder by the minute."

Lauren didn't know how to break it to him, but it

was going to get a lot weirder before they were all done, she feared.

"I know it's a lot to take in at once—"

"And why the hell did your cousin look like he wanted to kill me?"

Because he probably did, but she didn't think it would be very wise politically to point that out at the moment. Somehow, she needed to find a way to get Sebastian and Carson on a cooperative playing field, and Carson was going to be the easier party to persuade.

Maybe Carson's bit of witch blood, if nothing else, would soften Sebastian up with regard to helping him.

"Sebastian has seen too much. To say he's jaded would be a serious understatement."

"He has a grudge against mortals?"

"You would, too, if you spent your life trying to save witches from the wrath of them."

"So he basically operates an underground railroad for the witch community. Can't he tell I'm a friend?"

"The witch hunters are subtle and have managed to infiltrate witch circles enough times to make Gandhi suspicious. Sebastian is only doing his job by being hypervigilant."

"Vigilant is one thing. Looking like he wants to rip my head off is another. I don't care how powerful a witch he is, I'm not going to sit around and let him treat me like dirt."

"I'll talk to him. It might help that you're not a

pure-blood. It's actually kind of rare for a human to exhibit any witch trait."

"What's up with that tattoo, anyway? Why'd it disappear?"

"Sebastian is a shape-shifter. The raven can act as his eyes when he needs it to."

"Wow. Pretty cool talent to have."

"Trust me, I'm envious."

Carson leaned back on the bed, shaking his head in disbelief. "I thought I'd seen and done it all."

"You haven't seen the half of it."

"I guess that shape-shifting thing must come in handy during sex, huh?"

Lauren winced. "I try not to imagine my cousin having sex."

"You haven't been with any shape-shifters?"

There was that one guy in Paris, but Lauren thought it better not to mention such things to mortals. They tended to get intimidated.

"No. Against the rules. I've probably had more mortal lovers than witch lovers."

"And you see the future?"

Lauren nodded, not sure how much more she wanted to reveal about herself. It was a new sensation, this telling her secrets to humans thing. It was beyond strange. And although it was kind of liberating, it was also scary.

"Occasionally, I have visions." She'd briefly explained in the car earlier that she had premonitions, that her ability to predict the future on occasion was what set her apart from a mortal—along with her superior senses and heightened sexual abilities— but she had been purposely vague.

"And I'm in them?"

"I was lying to Sebastian," she lied.

No sense in giving Carson all the information. And she knew it wouldn't do any good for him to know he'd inhabited more than a few of her dreams and fantasies. It was no surprise he'd turned up in a vision, too.

Well, except… The surprising part was that her vision of him had happened before she knew him. Twenty-something years before she knew him, when she had been a little girl.

Lauren hadn't realized right away when she met Carson that he'd been the man in her vision. It had taken a recurrence of the vision last week, identical to the one she'd had as a child—and had had on occasion every few years or so since—of a man and woman running scared on a beach in the half darkness, for her to understand a least some of its significance.

The couple was her and Carson.

"Why'd you lie?"

"He trusts my visions. It was a way of getting him to let you stay at least for tonight. I'll have to do some more convincing to make him understand why he has to help us both."

Carson had his arms behind his head. He looked tired, like a guy who hadn't expected to get swept up in someone else's life drama on an otherwise dull

Tuesday night. Lauren felt a pang of guilt now for the first time. She had been so caught up in worrying about keeping them both alive that she hadn't stopped to consider how screwed this situation could make Carson's life.

How screwed it *would* make his life, because there really wasn't any turning back now.

His gaze half-lidded, he asked, "How do these visions of yours happen?"

"Sometimes I can will one to happen, and sometimes I can't. I can close my eyes and try to see some event from a different moment in time—usually the future, but sometimes I can get a vision from the past that I didn't witness. Sometimes it happens, but sometimes it doesn't."

"There's no rhyme or reason to it?"

"Witches are usually at their most powerful as children. Unless we practice and learn to harness that power, it fades with time. So as a kid, I could control it more than I can now."

"Why didn't you practice more?"

"I did practice as much as I could, but it was forbidden by the elders."

"Who are these elders you keep talking about?"

"It's our way of referring to the generation in power. They enforce the rules that have been handed down from antiquity, and they make new rules based on their own feelings about our time. The ruling generation is strictly opposed to the practice of our gifts."

"Wouldn't that help you defeat the people who

want to kill you, though, if you could do your super-natural stuff?"

"They took the opposite strategy. Practicing our gifts can draw attention and therefore can make us more vulnerable to being detected, so the elders decided to stop using their gifts generations ago. Mine was the first generation anyone can remember who decided to resist that rule."

"Why did you?"

Lauren stretched out on the opposite side of the bed, her tired body finally giving in to the need to relax. "Two things—my sister, and a vision I had."

He frowned, obviously perplexed by her cryptic answer.

"What was the vision?"

"I can't tell you right now," she said, her voice revealing her exhaustion, but when she saw his disappointment, she added, "but I will eventually."

"What about your sister? I didn't even know you had a sister."

She thought of pointing out that they knew almost nothing about each other. A shared Las Vegas fling may have taught them about each other's bodies, but their lives were still a mystery.

The thought of Carson's body caused her gaze to roam over him, and even now, she felt a warm buzz between her legs. They'd been amazing together. Explosive. Unforgettable.

And she had to get her mind as far away as possible from that particular train of thought.

She needed to adjust to the reality that she'd tumbled a few steps down on Maslow's Hierarchy of Needs, and now she was supposed to be in survival mode, not I-need-to-get-laid mode.

"I have a younger sister named Corinne. She's the most powerful witch alive, far as anyone knows, and she gave the younger generation the will not to suppress our powers completely. So we practiced in hiding. Even so, most of us have seen our powers fade over the years."

"How about Corinne's? Have hers faded?"

Lauren shook her head, a chill tingling along her spine at the strength of her sister's power. "Not one bit. She's amazing when she is disciplined about what she's doing."

"Why can't she just wipe out the witch hunters then?"

"I have no doubt she could, if only it were that easy. Corinne is still young, and quite the rebel. She's got a lot to learn about discipline before she'll be truly effective."

"So, you each have some different gift—what's hers?"

"She can command the natural world around her. The wind, the weather, fire, water, even animals will do her bidding."

"Wow. That's intense."

"We were once out hiking around in the hills near our family's house, and we accidentally wandered into the territory of a mountain lion. I froze in terror, but my sister just stared into the animal's eyes until it lay down and let us go without even the slightest aggressive gesture."

"But she can't do that kind of thing remotely?"

"No, she has to be within sight of the animal or element she wants to influence."

"Must be kind of hard, living in the shadow of such a powerful sister."

Lauren smiled. "I've never thought of it that way. She's my baby sister, three years younger than me. We grew up taking care of each other in a weird way. My mother was lost in her own world."

"So she wasn't the affectionate type?"

"She's a bitter, fearful woman. She never wanted to be a witch. She's always wished she was human, and while I don't blame her, I also don't see the point of ruining your life wishing for a different one."

"So she never practiced witchcraft?"

"Never. She is in charge of the family winery, and I think she was always horrified that my sister and I embraced being witches. It made us foreign to her."

"What about your father?"

"Witch families don't often include patriarchal figures in the way mortal families do. It's considered perfectly normal to have children with or without the paternal father sticking around to help raise the kids."

At the thought of kids—or more precisely the activity that made them—Lauren let her gaze roam over Carson's body. She wanted desperately to reach out and touch him, to forget everything else and ease the aching they both had to be feeling.

Running for her life wasn't supposed to make her horny. Her body wasn't supposed to be channeling her excess adrenaline into her libido. But it was. Then a wave of guilt hit her, because she'd endangered Carson's life, pulled him into a situation for which he had no coping skills, and here she was thinking about sex instead of thinking about the gravity of the situation.

"Do you even know your dad then?" Carson asked, jarring her out of her thoughts.

"I do. He lives in France, and we've visited him a few times. He's actually bisexual—which is pretty common among male witches—and living with a man now. I don't think he was ever comfortable with the idea that he had children with my mother. It wasn't exactly his style."

"Do witches live longer than humans?"

Lauren frowned. She'd never considered the matter before, oddly enough. "Sure, I guess so. I mean, I had a great-great-grandfather who lived to be like a hundred and five, but other than that, normal life spans."

"So back to the men thing. Where do they fit into the witch culture?"

"We grew up around uncles and grandfathers and such. It's just more casual, less structured as to who is a father figure for whom. I was close to one of my uncles—my mom's youngest brother Adrien who is an artist—and I guess he was like my father figure."

"Adrien Parish the San Francisco artist?"

"You know of him?"

"I saw one of his shows recently—the biomorphic cement installation pieces. Impressive stuff."

"He's amazing. Funny thing is, for the sake of the clan he's always tried not to achieve any kind of success or notoriety. He's made his art as unsellable and weird as possible just to stay out of the limelight, and that's what has started to bring him into it."

"I was given the assignment of finding a good piece of art for the lobby of the ad agency where I work. That's what I was doing combing the galleries. His stuff was definitely too weird for corporate America."

"So you got the big Bronson and Wade promotion, I heard. Congratulations."

"Pretty crazy when I wasn't even competing for it. Lucky for me Macy and Griffin left the agency."

Lauren smiled. During the infamous Vegas weekend Macy and Griffin had been competing for a promotion to Creative Director at the same advertising agency.

Instead of taking the prize job, they'd fallen in love, and decided to leave the agency to form their own firm. They'd been happy with the decision, even with all the stress and uncertainty of starting a new business at the same time they were starting a new relationship with each other.

In the aftermath, Carson had gotten the promotion, and Lauren had spent the past few months avoiding him at all costs. Now here they were, locked in a room together with nowhere else to go.

Life was crazy.

When she looked over at Carson again, she could see that he was struggling to stay awake. Under any other circumstances, sexual tension would be crackling between them, and knowing the two of them, they'd have been rolling around sweating and exchanging body fluids by now.

But these were no ordinary circumstances. It was nearly four in the morning, and their lives had been turned upside down, inside out and tossed against the rocks for good measure. They were both exhausted, and scared, among other things.

Likely they'd exchange body fluids again some other time, but not tonight. Lauren would have liked to think of herself as capable of maintaining an extra measure of self-control, for Carson's well-being, because the more he had her, the less other women would satisfy. Too bad she knew she couldn't. She wanted him almost as much as he wanted her, and soon enough, she would have him again.

She would have no choice. Her desires had been denied for too long.

Just when she thought he was asleep, he asked, his eyes still closed, "What does it feel like to have a vision? How does it happen?"

She tried to figure out how to describe it. She

closed her eyes and imagined. "I feel like I'm in a trance, like I'm concentrating really hard on something and I can't look away from it. And the images appear in my head."

"Tell me the truth. Was I really in one of your visions?"

She was so tired, the very act of closing her eyes had put her on the edge of a dream state, and she answered with her guard down, "Yes, we were in trouble. Running together on the beach, our lives in danger. That's how I know I have to protect you."

But she didn't tell him the rest. She didn't tell him that she had two kinds of visions, ones that came to her with a startling clarity—those were the ones she knew were real, that she couldn't change—and ones that came to her like a dream, fuzzy and weird. The second kind were always changeable. They were her chance to alter the future, to make a choice about her fate or someone else's.

She couldn't alter her and Carson's fate, though. She'd only had that one crystal clear vision of him, filled with a sense of fear, of impending doom. She had the burden of knowing he would witness her death on that cold beach at night. It had taken her years to understand that she was the woman in the vision, and that she'd been shown the moment of her own death.

Not exactly cheery news to walk around with, but she'd learned some things were bigger than herself. And she believed her death would serve an important purpose.

She was drifting off to sleep when she felt Carson take her hand in his. Her eyes fluttered open at the movement, and she saw him stretched out next to her, his hand holding hers. Not exactly the physical contact she'd been aching for, but still…nice.

Nice enough to chase away her fear for a little while.

This, she knew, might be the last time they'd ever feel even a little safe together.

5

HER MOUTH WAS ON HIM.

Kissing, licking, teasing. First his neck, then his shoulder, his bicep, his forearm, his fingers.

Oh yeah, his fingers. She was sucking them as if they were…

And then, his belly. And lower still. His cock strained, aching for the same attention. She didn't disappoint. Her hot wet mouth took him in, sucking gently, and he buried his hands in her silky hair and gasped at the mind-blowing sensations.

Carson could not remember when he'd wanted a woman so badly. "Lauren," he murmured. "Man, I've missed you."

Her fingertips trailed up his inner thigh, then over his balls, and she gripped him, massaging as she worked that magic with her mouth.

And then in an instant she was on top of him, straddling him, her naked, hot flesh only inches away. He grasped her hips, thrust into her tight, wet folds, realizing a moment too late that he hadn't bothered with a condom. He felt too damn frenzied to care.

This was the thing he lived for at this moment—being inside of Lauren, claiming her, having his way with her until she melted like butter on his cock. Until he spilled into her the way he'd fantasized about countless times in the past few months.

Their bodies slapped together as he thrust his hips and she moved in time with him. She was far better than he'd remembered. She felt too good to let go of again.

He was lost, and found, all at once.

Quickly, she reached her climax, and he held her heavy breasts in his palms and kissed her as she came. Her body contracted around him, wet and sated. He held her until she calmed, and then he thrust into her more fiercely than before. In a frenzy, he moved without thinking. Only feeling.

Over and over, again and again, until he, too, felt an orgasm coming on so strong he was powerless to slow it. The sensation hit him like a wall of water, and he rode it to its sweet, delicious end, overcome with the pulsing contractions.

More kissing, more caressing, more limbs tangled together. She was beside him, then under him, always against him—because he'd never let her get away.

He was delirious with the joy of finally having her again. So delirious he could feel tears on his cheeks, and he was not the kind of guy who ever shed a tear....

Carson opened his eyes, and he saw only the gray darkness of early morning. His eyes were dry. He was still dressed. His cock was hard and straining against his jeans. His mouth was parched and tasted bad. Lauren was not beneath him, but rather, as indicated by the sound of her breathing, she was on the other side of the bed.

Their hands were the only parts of their bodies still touching.

He whispered a curse to himself and ran his free hand over his face. He needed a shave, he decided as he yawned and stretched, finally letting go of Lauren.

He'd dreamed that entire episode. *Dreamed* was putting it mildly, though. It had been the most vivid, intense dream of his life. He rarely had sexual dreams anymore, and this one took the prize. For sure.

He felt as if he really had just had sex, his body was so full of sexual energy.

Then he noticed that Lauren wasn't sleeping soundly. Her breathing was fast and shallow, and growing more so. She was starting to move around on the bed. He sat up on his elbow and watched her in the darkness.

Her face held a slight tension, and her lips parted as she moaned softly and arched her back. Carson's dick strained harder.

Could she really have been experiencing the same kind of dream he had? Was this some kind of supernatural witch thing, to share sex dreams?

It took every ounce of his willpower not to unzip

his fly and mount her as he watched her moan and writhe. Her breath grew even shallower, until it sounded as if she herself was about to come.

Sweat broke out on his forehead, and he could feel himself leaking in his jeans.

Should he wake her and make love to her?

No, she wouldn't want that.

But watching her dream like this was the most erotic thing he'd seen in a long time. He wasn't sure how much more of it he could take before he'd have to get some relief.

He didn't have to wonder any longer. Her body tensed against the bed, her back arched harder, and she cried out the same way he remembered her sounding in Las Vegas when she came.

He watched, tortured, as the orgasm overtook her and her breathing slowed, then, finally settled to silence.

"Christ," he muttered, nearly insane with desire, and her eyes fluttered open.

She appeared disoriented for a moment, and then her gaze fixed on him.

"What…?" she said, her voice raspy.

"What just happened?"

"Yeah?"

"From my end, it looked to me like you came in your sleep."

She sat up on her elbow, frowning, and shuddered.

"Actually," she said slowly. "I did."

"Happen often?"

"No."

"I had a pretty erotic dream myself. Starring you, as a matter of fact."

She looked at him curiously. "You did?"

He nodded. "I don't think I got the grand finale you got, though," he said as he looked down at his erection.

"Wow."

"Is that some kind of witch thing? Shared erotic dreams?"

She lay back down and sighed heavily. "Um, yeah, I guess. I never thought of it as strictly a witch phenomenon, but I suppose it is. Maybe you were able to experience it because of your little bit of witch blood."

"Any idea how often this kind of thing happens? Because, you know, if we have to stay in close quarters and aren't allowed to touch each other—"

"We might go insane," she filled in.

"Well I will. I mean, at least you got yours in your dream."

She laughed and covered her face. "I don't know how often it happens. I think it's sort of a side effect of pent-up sexual energy."

"Great. I've got more than my share of that right now."

Carson dropped heavily onto his pillow, his cock stiff as ever, and the thought of going into the bathroom to take care of himself about as appealing as taking a sledgehammer to the problem.

This was going to be one long-ass stay at the Hotel Hell.

SEBASTIAN PARISH KNEW more than most people that trying to lose one's troubles in the flesh of a woman was a risky prospect, at best. For one thing, it might not have been a popular notion in the postmodern world, but as far as he could tell, women were by their very nature the embodiment of trouble. So even if one care might be forgotten through sex, a whole new storm of problems would be brewing.

But every once in a while, he would try again. Even now, with the pretty girl in the torn jeans and black tank top kneeling before him, his cock in her mouth, he knew he was doomed to fail.

In the dim morning light, he watched her red lips against his skin, watching her head bob back and forth as the sensation of her wet tongue and lips against him caused tension to coil inside him. He should have had an orgasm by now.

She'd been working on him for maybe a half hour, and while he was enjoying himself vaguely, he feared he wasn't going to come. But he didn't have the heart to tell her to stop, either. After working all night and into the morning, he should have been going to bed. The sun had risen, and this girl, left over from the crowd of revelers, had wandered into his office.

She was one of the lost ones. They came from everywhere, having heard he was powerful and that he provided a safe haven for witches who had nowhere else to go. He tried his best. But he felt lost, too, and he grew weary being everyone else's rescuer.

Who would rescue him? Certainly not this girl, with her probable drug habit and her reckless eyes. But somehow he had become the protector of every witch like her, the lost generation who'd been waiting for the powerful to rise up and lead them to a better life, free from fear.

Her mouth on his cock, he was not such a great protector. But he could see it in her eyes that she wanted to give him something back, and some heartless part of him wanted to oblige her in this small, selfish way.

Maybe… Maybe if he could close his eyes and imagine a different woman, a different set of circumstances…

He did. His breath quickened as he brought to mind the image of the woman he'd never wanted to love but who'd nonetheless haunted his dreams for months now.

Maia. Why did she always appear in his fantasies this way, when he wanted so badly to forget?

But it was Maia. Always Maia. He imagined her curly mane of hair, her impetuous smile, her small white teeth, her tiny, perfect breasts, her torso that snaked against the sheets, silky and warm beneath him.

Maia.

His breathing quickened more, and as he imagined plunging himself between her legs, imagined her here in this office with him, he felt his release coming. Faster, closer, almost there. Then, the rush of release, blinding white pleasure for a few moments, until it was gone.

He looked down at the girl, who was not Maia, and remorse flooded his chest, wiping away that momentary euphoria. This girl, like so many others, was nameless to him. Her dark brown hair was not Maia's, her slight, lovely body was not Maia's, and her warm, wet mouth was not Maia's.

A deep, crushing regret settled on his chest, and he nearly gasped for breath. But no, his lungs still worked, as did most of his other major organs. It was his heart, he suspected, that had died. Otherwise, how could he have done what he'd just done?

He stepped back from the girl as she stood and smiled coyly at him. She took a step closer, pressing her body to him, to kiss him, but he grasped her arms and said, "I'm sorry."

He leaned in and brushed her lips lightly with his, then set her aside. He tucked himself back into his jeans and zipped his fly.

"What?" she said, her eyes wounded.

"I shouldn't have."

"Oh." She had probably heard the stories, that this was what he did. That he never let anyone in, that he used women, that he was incapable of real intimacy.

But still, even with the rumors that floated around

the club about him, there were always women willing to offer themselves up as the one who might get through to him, who might reawaken his dead heart.

None could, yet he didn't always have it in him to turn them away.

"I'll go," she finally said, when he made no move toward her.

He nodded. "I'm sorry."

"Whatever." She opened a compact and checked her blood-red lipstick, which, remarkably, was only a little smeared.

A man with a heart would have taken her into his arms and kissed her, drawn her down to the desk and made love to her. But Sebastian wasn't that man and everyone knew it.

That knowledge didn't make him feel any less ashamed.

His physical need overcame him regularly, turned him into something he didn't want to be, but the need was still there. Always there.

"I'll go," she said, turning toward the door. "I have to work tonight."

Sebastian watched silently as she left the office. He'd given her a job serving drinks at the club a week ago, and she'd spent the time since stealing glances at him every chance she got. It was the burden he had, being a shape-shifter, knowing what people did behind his back. He always saw. He always knew, whether he wanted to or not.

A moment later, the door closed, and he was alone. On the wall, the clock read 8:10 a.m. And he thought of his cousin. She probably needed to sleep longer, but he doubted she'd really be asleep.

He went into the bathroom and cleaned up, and as he did so, he caught sight of himself in the mirror. He was starting to look like death. Like an addict, though he never used the drugs that some of the weaker witches used to mask their pain at being outcasts.

But sometimes it wasn't a drug or a disease that drove people close to death. Sometimes, he knew all too well, it was simply pain.

His eyes had gotten hollow, with purple shadows beneath, and he'd lost weight, giving his bone structure a disturbing prominence. His long black hair had gotten limp and greasy, and always looked that way no matter how often he washed it. It draped his shoulders like the cloak of a dead man.

And yet he had other things he needed to focus on besides his own self-indulgent pain. Lauren was in trouble. Lauren, whom he'd adored since childhood, whom he loved more than a sister. They'd grown up with the common bond of knowing death could seize them any moment they made a wrong move—a bond made all the stronger by the fact that they'd chosen to tempt fate by rebelling against the elders' rules.

He left the bathroom and headed upstairs to the room where he'd deposited Lauren and the mortal a few hours ago. He needed to talk to her while the mortal was still asleep. His anger flared at the thought of Lauren consorting with such an obviously smug, useless asshole.

Sebastian knew his cousin was too good for a mortal, but what could he say?

He'd have to think of something. He could not risk the danger of allowing a mortal to remain in their midst.

He stood outside the room about to knock on the door, when she opened it. She startled at the sight of him, then gathered her wits and covered her mouth with her finger to urge him not to speak. Over her shoulder, Sebastian could see the mortal still in bed sleeping.

Mortals were lazy—another of the ways they were inferior to witches, who only needed a few hours rest each day.

She closed the door behind her, and when they'd made their way down to Sebastian's office, she finally spoke.

"I need you to help Carson, too, and for more than just a day," she said, cutting straight to the issue.

She knew him too well. Sebastian bit his tongue. It wouldn't do any good to argue at the moment.

"Sit," he said, nodding at the chair across from his desk. "Tell me what you know about this mortal."

"First off, he's not totally mortal. He has some witch blood. I can see it in his palms."

Sebastian stared at her, unimpressed by the news.

"So what if his great-great-great-grandmother was part witch. He's still mortal."

"And he's also part witch. Our blood runs through him, too. Keep that in mind."

He shrugged. It didn't really matter to him. Anyone who'd grown up as a normal mortal knew nothing of the fear and persecution that came with being a witch.

"He's totally innocent, Sebastian. He's a friend of my best friend, and I know for a fact that he's not out to get us."

"How do you know that?"

"I just know. He's appeared in one of my visions, and I have the absolute feeling that he's someone I need to help me—and that I have to help him, too."

"I don't help mortals, Lauren."

"Do it for me."

A sick feeling settled in Sebastian's gut. He thought of the other mortals. Three had shown up here in the past two years, and he would have to tell her about them.

"The underground isn't the safe haven it once was, I'm afraid."

Lauren's eyes grew startled. "What do you mean?"

"I'm afraid The Order may be infiltrating. Three times, I've had mortals show up here in the past two years, and they were all one of them."

"Witch hunters? Found their way here? How?"

Sebastian shook his head. "I wish I knew."

"So what happened? How did you find them out?"

He said nothing, but she glanced at the raven tattoo on his arm and understanding dawned on her expression. "You saw."

"I don't know where they came from, or how they found us, but they did."

"But...what did you do?"

His gaze dropped to the surface of his desk. The truth many of their generation overlooked was that in facing down The Order, they had to also face that they had to kill, or be killed.

He leveled his gaze at her again. "I took care of the situation."

"You..."

"Killed them."

The color drained from her face. "But it's forbidden."

"A lot of what we do is forbidden. If we agree to break one of the rules of the elders, we are silently agreeing that it's okay to break them all, are we not?"

She leaned over and put her elbows on her knees, and covered her face with her hands. She wasn't crying, but he knew she was reeling. So was he, in his own way. It felt good somehow to hand the burden of his secret over to someone else, even if only for a moment.

"God, Sebastian. How did you— Where did you—"

"It's better if you don't know."

"Maybe the more important question is how they found this place. We have to figure that out."

"*We* don't have to do anything. You're on the run from The Order, so our first priority is keeping you safe from them. Let me worry about the other stuff."

"I'm such a goddamn fool," she said, and this time her voice broke, and she began to cry.

"We all are, in our own way."

"I'm sorry. I didn't realize I'd be endangering you by coming here."

"It's okay. It's my job to protect you," he said, but something in his voice sounded flat.

Dead.

She pulled herself together and wiped away the dampness in her eyes. "I can take care of myself," she said. "You have your own problems to worry about."

"Don't start talking like that. I'm not going to let you go off on your own and get yourself killed."

"I'm responsible for Carson's safety, and I won't let him down. So if you're not going to help him, too, I have no need for your help."

"You'd really let a mortal come between us?"

"It's not as simple as that, and you know it."

"It is, Lauren. We're family. Nothing, especially not some punk-ass mortal, should stand between us."

"He's a friend."

"More than a friend," he said, his gaze pinning her with his accusation.

"Yes, he's been my lover in the past."

He didn't feel jealousy, exactly. He thought of Lauren in the same way he would think of a sister. But he did feel a surge of protectiveness for her that verged on the irrational.

"Why?" he asked.

"You know why."

"I don't sleep with mortals."

"You've got access to a lot more witches than I do. You're surrounded by them. I, on the other hand, am surrounded by mortals every day."

He tried to put aside his distaste at the idea long enough to imagine himself in her situation. All he could imagine was being celibate. He didn't have the slightest desire for inadequate mortal flesh.

"I guess I'd have to be in your shoes to understand."

"You've seen the worst of humanity. You have a lot more reason to hate mortals than I do."

"Perhaps that's true."

"I worry about you. I think you let the hate consume you. You don't look so good, you know."

Sebastian thought of his own grizzly reflection and couldn't disagree. "Thanks, cousin."

"I mean, you look tired, and thin."

She didn't know about Maia. No one knew.

"What is it?" she asked.

He said nothing.

"The killings…are they weighing on you that much?"

He shook his head.

"Something else then…girl problems?"

He said nothing again, but her expression said she knew that she'd nailed the truth.

"Who?"

"You don't know her."

"What happened?"

"One of the mortals—she led him here. He was her lover, and she came here for protection, but she didn't realize he was the one she needed protecting from."

"So you killed the guy."

"I did, and she hated me for it. She thought I was a monster after that."

"Where did she go?"

"I had to send her away. Gave her a new identity, helped her get started in Miami. I haven't heard from her since."

"But you fell in love with her?"

Sebastian stared at the black, scuffed surface of the desk again. "I don't know why. I just looked at her and thought I saw my home."

"She didn't return the attraction?"

"In a weird way, I think she sort of did. Which made her want to get away from me even more after what had happened with the mortal."

"She thought you were motivated by jealousy."

He nodded. "Maybe I sort of was. But I had to kill him, regardless."

"What was her name?"

"Maia," he choked out before it could catch in his throat. He hadn't said her name aloud in a long time.

"I've never seen you like this over a woman. How long has it been?"

"Eight months."

"It'll get better," she said, but her eyes still looked worried.

"Don't worry about me. Right now we need to think about where you should go."

"Given my choice, I want to stay here with Carson."

"No. That's out of the question."

Lauren leaned forward in her chair, resting her elbows on her knees again, and she looked at him the way she did when she wasn't going to change her mind.

"You need help right now, and I can help you."

"No, you can't."

"Maybe what we need is to lead the guys who are after me right here, so we can capture them and get information about The Order. This could be the opportunity we've been waiting for."

"I'm not going to risk your safety like that. Someone else can be a decoy, but not you."

"My visions have been getting more frequent. Corinne thinks that means something."

Sebastian wanted to argue further, but at the mention of Corinne he went silent. His little cousin, of any witch on Earth, would know.

"What else did she say?" he finally asked, but he was torn between feelings of dread and curiosity.

The curiosity, he understood, but the dread gave him pause. Why? The answer came to him in an instant. All these years of hoping and looking forward to the uprising, he'd never considered the very real possibility that they might not succeed in it. He'd never considered that Lauren's vision of their future might be wrong, or that they had all their hopes pinned o a pipe dream.

He'd never considered it, and he wouldn't start now. They had no choice but to succeed.

6

OCCASIONALLY, LAUREN envied the power her sister's name evoked. Mention of Corinne Parish was enough to send any witch of her generation into reverent silence. But with that considerable power came a huge burden, one Lauren didn't envy at all. She'd never aspire to be the savior of an entire generation.

And as a big sister entirely too familiar with Corinne's personality, Lauren wasn't sure she wanted that burden to fall on her wild, impetuous younger sibling, either. But it was the way it was. It was the way it had always been.

Corinne, for her part, didn't seem to mind. She was too headstrong and full of herself to slow down and consider the weight of her burden or think about the consequences her every decision had.

Lauren stared into Sebastian's bloodshot eyes, and she knew she absolutely was not going to leave him here alone. He needed her help, whether he realized it or not, and she was going to find a way to give it.

"Corinne said she was beginning to feel like it was time. Like the season was coming."

"The season?"

"That's how she's started describing the uprising."

He nodded. "Makes sense, I guess."

Corinne's ability to control nature was stunning to the uninitiated. She could command the weather to change in an instant, shift the ocean tides, summon the wind, bring the animals to heel at her side. Hers was the rarest of powers among witches, because in harnessing the natural world, she could increase her own strength until almost nothing could stop her. An awesome power in the hands of someone who tended not to think before acting. This was compounded by the fact that the purity and intensity of her gifts were at levels higher than any witch anyone could remember.

The elders only had an inkling of how strong Corinne really was. If they'd known the truth... Lauren could not allow herself to think about what might have happened.

On top of her other activities, Corinne had a sense of intuition that was uncanny. While all witches were intuitive, Corinne could take any situation and foresee its logical conclusion more quickly than anyone Lauren had ever known. When her little sister said something was going to happen, it happened.

"What else did she say?"

"Only that I should keep myself ready to act, not go too far."

"So that's why you really want to stay here? You think Corinne will want us all together when it starts happening."

It. The event they'd all been fantasizing about their entire lives.

"Yes," Lauren said. "She will."

"We've been living on the edge for so long, it's hard to believe the revolution we've been waiting for might finally happen."

"Tell me about it. I feel like it's become this unattainable dream. Despite wanting it so much, I've almost accepted it will never really happen. Now even the suggestion that it's imminent freaks me out a little."

Sebastian nodded. "Have you ever tried to imagine how it will go down? What our lives will really be like after?"

"I've always imagined that we'd experience real freedom to be truly ourselves… But maybe that's a little naive."

"Why do you say that?"

"Because in my mind I too often skip over the hard part—the actual uprising. I don't know how it will go or how long it will take."

"Your vision only told you it would be successful, right? No other details?"

Lauren nodded. "Yeah. I saw us celebrating victory against The Order." It had happened so long ago without recurring that the image was fuzzy to her now.

And she sometimes worried that, because it had not recurred, it was perhaps a faulty vision, that her longing for a successful uprising had sparked it rather than insight into actual future events. But she could not let those fears dissuade them from what had to be done.

"I've thought about how to defeat The Order. We'd have to infiltrate it and bring it down from within, but they're worse than the CIA when it comes to security."

"No easy task, that's for sure. How would witches get in without being detected? I guess we could use mortals but how could we trust that The Order didn't brainwash them?" Lauren sighed. "I don't doubt we can do it, but it's such a huge maneuver it overwhelms me."

"I hear you, but we have to hope Corinne will be up for it. Even if the rest of us aren't."

"You're right," Lauren said. She did want to believe they had a future in which they could live openly as witches without fear.

It occasionally struck her as odd to think of her baby sister launching a revolution—especially a baby sister as out of control as Corinne. Lauren was too familiar with the varied aspects of Corinne's personality—too often had witnessed her being impulsive or selfish or stubborn—to see only the leader who would guide them to victory. But then again, they'd know Corinne would take charge since their childhood. The basic plan they'd hatched in the hills near the vineyards under the cypress trees had never changed in all these years.

Sebastian studied Lauren intently before seeming to come to a decision. "Only because you say your vision includes the mortal, I will let him stay here for now. But the first time he crosses me or takes any unnecessary risk, I will remove him. His life doesn't matter to me."

Lauren's stomach clenched at his words. Sebastian had changed since she'd seen him last. Something in him had hardened. And even though his earlier confession should have warned her, she now fully understood he was capable of things that she was not.

"Thank you," she said. "I owe you my life."

At least she had time to figure out how best to aid Sebastian, how best to protect Carson and how best to help defeat The Order. For the first time since she'd heard the men outside her door, she felt as though she had some tiny measure of control.

And with this reprieve Sebastian had granted, she knew she walked a fine line where Carson was concerned. Now, more than ever, she had to deny her desire for him so as not to piss off Sebastian and give him justification to *remove* Carson. Lust and concern for him battled within her. She only hoped that Carson did nothing to tip the lust advantage because she wasn't convinced she could resist him.

CARSON WOKE UP with another raging, rock-hard erection. Or perhaps the one he'd gotten earlier had never gone away. Entirely and frustratingly possible.

At least he hadn't been plagued by any more unful-filled erotic dreams. A guy could only take so much.

He stared down at his dick straining against his jeans and struggled to think past his sexually charged state to remember where he was and why he felt as though he needed to sleep for another ten hours or so.

There was also the simultaneous need to piss. An ache so deep he felt as if he hadn't gone to the bathroom in ages.

He blinked in the morning light, and as soon as the fog began to lift from his brain, he remembered why his erection was so damn urgent. Lauren. Lying next to him. He looked over at where he thought she would be, but no one was there.

The rumpled cover and pillows on the other side of the bed told him that his night sleeping in the same bed with her hadn't been a cruel dream, but the room was silent. When he turned his head, he spotted a note on her pillow.

Be back soon. Gone to find breakfast. LP.

Her handwriting was small and exact, the writing of a scientist. Not a flight attendant. Man, he must have been blinded by sex that weekend to have ever believed that she was anything but a brilliant re-searcher. If he'd bothered to look past her hot bod and actually listened to her, he would have known she was way more intelligent than she pretended to be. But no, he'd been too focused on getting her on her back—and against the wall, and straddling him—again that he hadn't seen the holes in her story.

Before his mind replayed a selection of his favorite steamy memories from that weekend, Carson got out of bed. He stumbled across the room, his tired body not quite ready yet to give up its fight to get some rest, and made his way to the bathroom where he relieved himself. Then he stretched, splashed some water on his face, and went back out to the bed to take stock of his situation.

He'd slept in his clothes, which were now rumpled but probably good for wearing another day. Besides, he had nothing else to wear. The room had a phone, but no television or computer. He did have his cell phone, too, although he'd been instructed not to turn it on or call anyone.

So he was stuck here until Lauren returned. And he was still damn tired. He stretched out on the bed again and closed his eyes, figuring he'd probably need all the rest he could get if they had to be on the run again soon.

But his mind wouldn't quiet down. He wasn't sure what to make of all the witch stuff—the magic and the secrets and all that—but he wasn't finding himself feeling all that skeptical, either. And it did explain why Lauren was so much more thrilling to him than any mortal woman.

Because she wasn't mortal.

He laughed to himself at the thought.

Then a sound at the door silenced him, and he sat up on his elbow as Lauren reentered the room. She looked refreshed in the morning light, in a way that Carson distinctly did not feel. Her skin was luminous, her eyes bright as she took in the sight of him.

"Hey," she said. "I brought breakfast."

He then noticed the two bags in her hand. She crossed the room, and on the table next to the window, she took out two covered cups of coffee and two pastries.

"You went out?"

She shook her head. "Sebastian brought us some stuff."

"You talked to him?"

"Yes, he's agreed to let us stay here for now, until we have a better plan."

"But what does that even mean? Do you have any way of catching the guys who are after you?"

Lauren sipped her coffee and frowned. "I have some memory of what they look like. I think I'm going to put all the information into a computer database that we have about The Order, including physical descriptions of those men."

"Maybe you could get an artist's rendering of them."

She nodded. "Sebastian can draw very well. I'll ask him to do it."

Carson took a bite of his pastry, a chocolate croissant, and realized for the first time how hungry he was.

"So what else can we do? We can't just sit here. Can't you get the police involved or something?"

She already said no to calling the police last night in the car, but he couldn't help asking again. It just seemed insane that there were murderous thugs after them, and they had to battle them on their own.

"No, we never involve the police," she said, as if it were perfectly logical not to.

"Doesn't Sebastian have some idea of what you should do? I thought he was the big protector guy."

"He would have me take a new identity and leave the country, but he's overreacting out of protectiveness."

"I want to help, however I can," Carson said.

Lauren frowned. "For now, we just sit tight and stay out of sight. I'll keep talking to Sebastian until we have a better plan."

Easier said than done. Carson thought of his erection, which was back in a big way now that Lauren was in the room, and the crazy-lucid dream they'd shared last night. He craved her just as strongly as he had before, only now there was all this intrigue and danger and denial that should have been tempering his libido.

But his dick didn't care about witches or witch hunters. His dick only cared that Lauren was in the room, and that she was the most arousing woman he'd ever met, and that the dream he'd had last night was a vivid reminder of how amazing she was in bed.

He smiled. "I'm sure we'll think of something to do."

"SHE WON'T BE EASY to catch."

"No, she's left San Francisco by now, I'm sure."

Lars Klein stared out the window of Lauren Parish's apartment at the gray San Francisco day. Fog hung low in the air, giving the afternoon a chill and a damp scent of sea air. They'd combed every inch of the apartment twice, considering every bit of information a clue to the witch's possible whereabouts.

The video camera they'd left behind when they'd pursued her had given them the image of a man entering the doorway of her apartment for a moment, but nothing else. They didn't know if he was a witch or a mortal, and they had no idea who he was to Lauren Parish.

His partner Noam was reading files on the computer, making note of names and addresses.

Lars did not hate witches. His purpose in life was to kill them, but not to hate them. His father, and his father's father, and all the Kleins who had come before, had been witch hunters. He had been born into the calling, so to speak.

He'd been raised in the secret society known only as The Order, and for as long as he could remember, he had been taught that his purpose in life was to rid the world of witches, because they upset the natural order.

Some tried to claim it was a battle between good and evil, or a struggle between morality and immorality. The truth was simply a matter of keeping nature in balance. That was the ultimate purpose of The Order, as Lars saw it, and anything more was a bastardization of the truth.

"She's been careful," Noam muttered. "I'm not finding much in the way of personal contacts on her computer. Just food delivery places, a dry cleaner, crap like that."

Lars turned from the window and surveyed the disheveled room. They'd torn the place apart, and by now, it seemed they'd found everything they were going to find.

"She could be across the border into Mexico now, or on a plane to Europe for all we know."

"But we're assuming she's one of them," Noam said as he closed the laptop. Lars watched as the younger man packed it in a case to take with them.

"I think it's a safe assumption. She fled faster than any mortal would have, and she didn't call the police."

Not that it would have made a difference if she had. The Order had been evading the police's lackadaisical eye for too long to find them even the slightest deterrent to their mission.

"The family resemblance thing has been a false lead before."

"Lauren Parish has the eyes of a witch. There's

something hard in those eyes that I've never seen in a mortal. It's the hardness that comes with the knowledge that one has power over other people," Lars said.

"Let her goddamn powers save her now."

The two men gathered up the last few things they wanted to take from the apartment, then slipped out. Their plumbers' uniforms were a safe decoy in case they ran into any neighbors, but they exited the building without being spotted.

Five minutes later, they were sitting in their van, studying a map of California.

"There's one obvious place for a witch to go in this state," Lars muttered, as he eyed the southern portion of the state.

"L.A."

Lars nodded. "West Hollywood. If she's anywhere…"

"I'll bet she's there."

They'd only recently begun to crack the underground network that seemed to exist around the famous neighborhood that was known more as a place to look for stars than anything else. What was hidden beneath the glitz and tourist bustle was a labyrinth witch haven.

Gaining access to it without getting killed was a challenge in itself, but The Order was making progress. The Order didn't have the advantage of supernatural powers, but the most skilled of their hunters, Lars among them, had keen senses of intuition that could detect witch from human. It helped that witches often had distinctive physical beauty that set them apart from humans. But mostly The Order relied on traditional spy methods to seek out the witches, and when necessary, DNA testing to positively identify them. The Order was experimenting with technologies that helped them differentiate the electro-magnetic fields that were created when witches used their supernatural powers.

This generation of witches had proven to be their first real challenge in centuries. Instead of cowering, some of these younger witches had chosen to fight back. More frequently than ever before, members of The Order had been killed trying to track down their prey.

Who had done the killing, they didn't know. They only knew that they were getting close to something big, and it would take skill and patience to find the truth.

Lauren Parish, with her carelessness, might lead them right where they needed to go, if they were lucky. And Lars, for all his years of witch hunting, had come to know that luck was always on his side.

To be a hunter was to understand when he had to let go of reason and rely on the senses, to follow his animal instincts just as quickly as he followed his intellect. Lars, born of The Order, was above all else a hunter.

He would hunt down Lauren Parish, with her cold, unrelenting beauty and her steely eyes, and he would take her. He would show her just how little power she had, and then he would rid the world of her for good. His cock stirred at the thought.

They headed toward 19th Avenue, which would take them south, out of the city, and he could only suspect, closer to their prey.

7

THE NIGHTCLUB WAS EMPTY, but a Nine Inch Nails song still pumped from the speakers, and overhead strobe lights flashed. Lauren had never lain down on the dance floor, and she was surprised how clean it was, how smooth and shiny.

But then Carson was on top of her, mounting her, and she forgot about the floor against her naked flesh. She gasped as he penetrated her, stretching and pushing into her where she ached most. Wrapping her legs around his hips, she pulled him closer until he filled her all the way.

"Closer"… That was the name of the song playing, she recalled in a haze as he claimed her mouth and thrust his tongue in.

She dug her nails into his hard shoulders, and she returned his fierce kiss with her own. Her muscles were coiling so tightly around his cock, it was all she could do to hold on to the edge without letting herself come so soon.

So fast. It was happening so fast. They were sweating…a pool of it forming between her breasts, and on her belly. His sweat and hers, mingled together.

He felt too good inside of her. So good she couldn't imagine this ending, couldn't imagine letting go.

Why were they on the dance floor? And where was everyone? The questions faded as he pumped into her faster.

She watched his face, dark and intense, his gaze locked on hers, never looking away, and she wondered why she'd wanted to hold off. She couldn't imagine saying no to this ever again.

So what if they were lost? So what if their lives were ruined? So what if they died tomorrow, as long as they had each other right now?

Inside her, his cock grew stiffer, harder, and he pressed deeper into her as he neared climax. He was hitting her in just the right spot…so right…so good…she was almost there…

He cried out as he spilled into her, and she let herself go with him. She came hard, her body overcome, her every nerve stimulated.

And then she was in a dark room. Lauren blinked, looking around. The hotel room. The clock radio read 5:00 a.m.

Her body was drenched with sweat, and between her legs, she was aching, throbbing, just on the other side of orgasm. She took a deep breath and sank heavier into her pillow.

What the hell?

It had all been a dream? Again?

Damn it.

She looked over at Carson, who was breathing fast, stirring in his sleep, his left hand grasping at the sheet and his brow furrowed in concentration. He must have been having the dream, too, and she wanted in the worst way to wake him up and make that dream a reality.

No.

She had to be good. Had to practice restraint. Had to keep her eye on the matter at hand. Dealing with The Order. That was her purpose in life now, wasn't it?

She wiped at the sweat on her forehead, and then she decided she needed a long, cold shower. But she couldn't risk waking up Carson and making this night even more difficult to get through.

So instead, she rolled over, putting her back to him, and closed her eyes, praying she could make the rest of the night without dreaming.

LAUREN'S EYES had started to glaze over as she sat at the desk, keying in information, trying her best to distract herself from Carson. It was their second day stuck inside Sebastian's hotel, and their second day recovering from a night of intense erotic dreams. She wasn't all that accustomed to having orgasms in her sleep, and the experience was oddly unsatisfying. It left her aching for sex in a way that normal desire did not. It was a bone-deep kind of aching.

Carson had been in the shower for a while now, and when he came back into the bedroom and stood near her, the ache intensified even more. The fresh, clean smell of him had lust pounding so hard in her veins she almost didn't hear him when he spoke.

"Where did you get the computer?"

"Borrowed it from Sebastian."

"What are you doing?" Carson said as he peered over her shoulder at the computer screen.

She wanted to grab him and screw him like an animal. She wanted his mouth on her body, on all the places that were throbbing.

"I figured if we're stuck here, we might as well be doing something productive, so I'm entering all the new information I have into the database we have about The Order."

"You know how to do that?"

"I'm a scientist. I know a few things," she said. "But it's really as simple as keying in data—nothing complicated."

"Right. I keep forgetting you aren't actually a flight attendant."

He poked her in the ribs, and she laughed even as her body responded to the physical contact. But a pang of guilt hit her in the stomach. She really regretted the lies she told mortals, but something about Carson made her crave honesty. "I'm sorry for lying to you," she said. "I hope you can understand now why I had to."

"Sure. Besides, it was Vegas. I'm the fool for

even thinking you'd give me your real name. I think I was thrown off because Macy was involved, and I didn't think she'd have any reason to lie to me."

"You were right about that. But that's best friends for you. Even if she didn't agree with me lying to you, she never questioned me about why."

"Will you ever be able to tell her the truth?" Carson said, pulling up a chair at the desk beside her and watching as she typed.

She felt another pang of guilt. What was it with these mortals lately? "I'd like to but I doubt it. At least not any time soon."

"Not until after the uprising?"

"Right."

She was a bit surprised she'd told Carson about the witches' plan to stop living in secret and let the world know they existed for real. But then again, she'd been so desperate to distract him—and herself—from thoughts of sex, she would have said just about anything.

Part of her desperately wanted to sleep with him again—apparently the part that controlled her dreams—while another part of her felt a crippling fear of pissing off Sebastian by sleeping with Carson in this place and giving him all the reason he needed to get rid of Carson. Plus there was that issue of sexual addiction. Right there was a chance—albeit a small one—that he'd be able to return to his normal life. If she seduced him again and he became obsessed all over, he would probably stop at nothing to see her again. And now that The Order most likely knew of his connection to her, he would lead them right to the witches' doorstep.

Still, having Carson this close was a distraction, to say the least, and she could tell their physical closeness had a strong effect on him, too. She wanted to back away, to make things easier on him, even while she wanted to forget all the reasons they shouldn't be together.

Lauren glanced back at the computer screen, at the sobering information about The Order, and reminded herself why they were here. Not for sex, but to save their lives.

Carson may not have understood yet how much the course of her life would be altered from now on, but she did. She was losing her old life. Now that she'd been identified, the chances that she could return to her life were remote. She couldn't let herself think about it too much or she'd be overcome with rage and sadness. Until the uprising, she'd have to build a new network of friends and lovers, seek out a new occupation, find a new reason to exist. And it would include defeating The Order.

If she was able, she'd also make sure Carson could return to his old life. But that had to be a secondary goal now.

"I can't believe such blatant racism is happening in America today, right under everyone's noses."

Lauren looked at him, and she had to resist the urge to lean in and kiss him. That he could grasp the root of the issue so quickly and not get sidetracked by the distraction of the witches' supernatural powers said a lot for him.

"Our powers do complicate things," she said. "It gives people more to fear."

"Fear comes from ignorance, though," he said. "Don't you think that if everyone understood your powers, they'd be more tolerant?"

"I wish, but the Salem Witch Trials weren't that long ago."

"Yeah, but those were the freaking Puritans doing the persecuting. What do you expect?"

She smiled. "That's why most of us witches live in large, liberal cities now. We figure if we're ever found out, we're more likely to be accepted as normal."

"I'm sorry you have to live like this. The more I think about it, the angrier I get."

Lauren turned away from the computer and studied his expression. "You're serious, aren't you?"

"What? Of course I am."

"Thank you for caring. I have to admit I never expected a mortal to give a damn one way or the other."

"Then you're not giving people enough credit. I'm sure there are lots of us who will care."

"It's hard to think that way, since history has proven otherwise."

"We live in more progressive times now. There will always be narrow-minded people, but I'll bet whenever you finally come out of the closet as a race, you're going to meet with more acceptance than you might expect."

She shook her head. "I can't imagine. The Order has made it hard for us to feel anything but paranoia."

"Those bastards need to be brought down. I'll do whatever I can to help."

"It wouldn't be fair to get you more involved than you already are. You'd be in even more danger."

"It should be my choice whether or not I want to put myself in danger for a cause I care about."

He looked and sounded dead serious. Lauren found herself reeling from the rush of emotion toward this man. During that weekend when she'd taken him in every conceivable way, she would have never expected him to have this sense of outraged justice, never expected him to volunteer to slay her demons. The heroism in his words humbled her and moments passed before she was able to speak past the tightness in her throat.

"Why do you care so much?" she asked.

"I care about what happens to you, for one thing. And for another, I can see you're a whole race of people in trouble. Why wouldn't I care?"

She shrugged. "You barely know me." Her answer served as a reminder. She needed to rein in her spiraling emotions. He was a mortal. She was a witch. Their lives were in danger. There was no room for sex or, God forbid, romance in this situation.

He went silent and seemed to be staring at a spot on the desk that wasn't there. She desperately wanted to reach out and touch his strong jaw. She couldn't help imagining what that soft brown stubble would feel like against her face, her breasts, her belly….

The aching between her legs was too much, demanding attention, demanding release. She shifted in her seat, trying to will her thoughts back to safe territory.

When he finally spoke again, he said, "I guess racism is more of a hot-button issue for me than I realized. I had to think for a while to figure out why."

"Why is it?"

"I dated a woman for a few years in my twenties. We were in love, and we were getting serious about each other. I was thinking of proposing to her, actually."

"What happened?"

"My parents disapproved of the fact that she was African-American. They were friendly enough to her when they thought she was just another girl I was dating, but when I told them I was thinking about getting married to her, they flipped out."

"Wow, I'm sorry."

"I tried not to let their opinions affect me, but I have to admit, their reaction made me hesitate. Then she found out about my parents' feelings and she broke up with me."

"That must have been rough." But Lauren felt a secret pang of relief that he hadn't gotten married in his twenties, because then she never would have met him.

Except, their meeting had gotten him into trouble with her. She knew she wasn't supposed to be glad to have Carson around. It was just kind of hard to remember why when she wanted to do him so badly.

"As far as the relationship went, breaking up was for the best, I guess. We were young and dumb, and probably wouldn't have gone the distance. But I've always been ashamed that I might have let my parents' racist opinion sway me even a little."

"Don't be too hard on yourself. You probably hesitated because you knew what a difficult life you'd be bringing her into, with in-laws who didn't like her. And what would that have meant for any kids you might have had? It would have been hard on them, too."

"None of that is any excuse. I promised myself I'd never be swayed by racism again, and maybe that's why I feel so strongly now about your cause…and you."

Lauren considered his words. None of it was any excuse? Had she been trying to justify to herself why she didn't want to deal with the complications of getting more involved with Carson?

She didn't want to think about their relationship now. The layers upon layers of problems they were dealing with were all making her head hurt.

Carson shifted his leg, and it bumped against her, sending a chill through her body that was far too intense for a mere brushing of body parts. The screaming of her libido overshadowed their present situation and reminded her that she seriously needed to get laid.

"So do you get along with your parents otherwise?" she asked, hoping to distract herself from any more thoughts of sex.

But Carson was studying her, and he didn't answer right away. Instead, he said, "When I brushed up against you, you reacted, didn't you?"

"What do you mean?"

"Your nipples got hard."

She glanced down at her traitorous nipples. "It's a little cold in here."

"It just suddenly got cold when my leg bumped you?"

Lauren rolled her eyes. "Oh stop."

"You're hot for me. Admit it. Those sex dreams we've been sharing aren't cutting it, are they?"

She tried not to laugh but failed. "I told you that witches are highly sensual. We're more sexually responsive than mortals."

"I noticed. I suspect you've gotten to come the past two nights, while all I've gotten is rock-hard."

"And yes," she admitted before she could stop herself. "I am very attracted to you. That doesn't hurt."

Or it did. Or something.

"You're crazy if you think we can stay cooped up in this hotel room without having sex."

"I'll make sure Sebastian gets you your own room as soon as one's available."

"If you want me to stay in this crazy-ass place, we're sleeping in the same room."

"What is that? Some kind of threat?"

Carson shrugged, his eyes sparkling with mischief. "Maybe."

"Are you saying that if I don't sleep with you, you won't stay within the safety of Sebastian's protection?"

"Not exactly, but now that you mention it, yes. That's what I'm saying."

"That's not fair," she said lamely.

"I'm sorry. I'll give you a bit of time to consider my offer. How's that?"

She glared at him but said nothing, and unlike other mortals who might have cowered under her cold glare, Carson simply smiled as if he knew he'd won the battle before it had even gotten started.

CARSON WAS STARTING to learn how to push Lauren's buttons, and he was having far too much fun with his newfound knowledge. If he was going to be tortured by agonizingly good sexual dreams at night without getting any satisfaction from them, he needed to find some kind of entertainment for himself during the day.

When he'd seen Lauren working at the laptop, it reminded him that he hadn't once thought about work since he'd arrived in L.A. His work, which he'd once claimed to be his all-consuming passion and his reason for not getting involved with anyone, hadn't even crossed his mind.

Admittedly, having a woman as gorgeous as Lauren around was a good way of giving a guy a brand-new all-consuming passion. But still, he was the creative director of a major ad agency. He was supposed to be running the show, and he hadn't even spared a thought for the job.

That was when he knew he didn't really give a damn about his work. And for a moment he felt without purpose, as though his life had been an elaborate forgery.

"To answer your question about my parents, no, we don't get along much anymore. I don't think I ever forgave them completely for their reaction to my girlfriend back then."

"You have any siblings?" Lauren said as she stood and stretched.

He tried to focus on her words, but instead the sight of her long lean torso distracted him. Her little black top pulled up as she stretched, exposing the pale smooth skin of her belly above the waist of her jeans. He wanted desperately to touch her there, to slide his tongue over her. She followed his gaze and then tugged her top down in a hurry.

"Behave yourself," she said with a little smile.

"What did you say?"

"Siblings. Do you have any?"

"An older brother and a younger sister. They're both closer to my parents than I am and still live within a few minutes of the family McMansion in Woodside."

"The family McWhat?"

"McMansion—you know, one of those stucco monstrosities that everyone around here seems to aspire to own. A big-ass house with too many bedrooms and too many bathrooms and a pool in the backyard."

"Oh right. I forgot you were a spoiled little rich kid like me."

"Your family strikes me as old money. Mine's all new money from some smart real estate investments my dad made back in the seventies."

"Yeah, the wine business has been in my family for centuries," Lauren said. "First in France and now here. I guess that counts as old money."

"I would think with all that money would come some power to defeat The Order," Carson said.

The amount of anger he felt toward an organization he hadn't known existed until a few days ago surprised him. Pure outrage filled him to think that there were people dedicating their lives to hunting down and killing people like Lauren.

She shrugged. "You would think, but I guess the thing about the witch clan is that we've had to live in fear for so long, we've let the fear control us."

"I guess I can see how that would happen. Like you said, witch hunting isn't exactly a new thing."

She regarded him curiously. "Why aren't you afraid of us?" she asked.

Good question. Carson wasn't sure he knew the answer, but in his gut, he just knew Lauren wasn't someone to fear. Her cousin Sebastian, however, was another matter entirely.

"I've always believed in trusting my gut about people, and my gut tells me you won't harm me."

"Your gut hasn't really dealt with the supernatural before, though. And, I haven't harmed you. Remember that obsession thing."

He shook his head. "Whatever that was it didn't hurt me. I could sense from the start that there was something different about you, something that set you apart from other women."

"Well, thank you for trusting me. It makes things a little less complicated, at least for now."

Carson watched her walk across the room and peer out the window, and his entire body ached to follow her and take her into his arms. He wanted to throw her on the bed and bury himself in her the way he had in the dance floor dream, until all the damn aching stopped.

Sadly he also knew that probably wouldn't go over very well at the moment. Soon enough though, he'd convince her, damn the consequences.

He wasn't afraid of a big bad addiction, not if it meant having Lauren in his bed again. Now that he was beginning to understand how little he was missing his job—how little he was missing his entire life, actually—he realized he had nothing to lose by going after Lauren with everything he had. A woman as amazing as her overshadowed everything else he'd thought mattered to him. She made the rest of it seem as meaningless as it really was.

8

HANGING AROUND with a bunch of witches was driving Carson to drink. He and Lauren weren't allowed to go out anywhere, and, since she had yet to take him up on his not-so-subtle offers of sex, their only entertainment was the nightclub. Which was where he sat now, feeling the slightest bit out of place.

Sebastian wasn't helping matters. As he served drinks, he took every opportunity he had to glare at Carson as if he wanted to snap his neck. Enough was enough already. Finally, while Lauren was in the restroom, Carson decided to confront her cousin.

Sebastian set the drink Carson had ordered in front of him, letting some of it slosh onto the bar, and his expression challenged Carson to say something.

"What's your problem?" he asked casually.

"You," Sebastian answered.

"Look, man, I appreciate your letting me stay here. I know you're only doing it as a favor to Lauren—"

"I don't want your thanks, mortal. I want you the hell away from my cousin."

"That's her choice, don't you think?"

The raven on Sebastian's arm fluttered its wing, and Carson glanced down at it.

"You're lucky you have a drop of witch blood, or I would have already killed you for sleeping with Lauren."

The fact that Sebastian's tone was chilling, without a hint of rage, made his words seem more dire. Carson grabbed his courage with both hands, refusing to let this guy get the advantage. "Is that a threat?"

"Call it whatever you want. Just understand that if I have the chance, I will not hesitate to take your life." And with that, Sebastian turned on his heel and went to the other end of the bar.

Carson watched him and sipped his drink, his male ego urging him to jump over the bar and settle their dispute with his fists. But he knew he was on shaky ground, in a nightclub full of witches with supernatural powers. The odds were not in his favor so there wasn't a hell of a lot he could do.

He downed the last of his Johnnie Walker Black and winced at the familiar, smooth burn as it went down. Not even the best whiskey—or Sebastian's promise of retribution—could rid Carson of the intense need that got worse every time Lauren was near. How the hell was he supposed to stay in that tiny room with a woman who was the best kind of addiction, and yet never get to fulfill his need? Absolute insanity.

He watched her return to the bar, where she stood at the far end talking to her jerk-ass cousin. Just watching her mouth and his cock went stiff in his jeans again. Something had to give—preferably Lauren, and preferably tonight.

No more of her goddamn excuses, and to hell with Sebastian's threats. He was either going to have Lauren hot and willing underneath him, or he was outta here.

A sly-looking blonde watched Carson from a few feet away, but he kept his expression blank and turned his attention back to Lauren. She stopped talking to her cousin and caught his eye, then came toward him.

"Hey," she said when she'd made her way through the growing crowd. "You're still here."

"The thought of going back to the room isn't exactly thrilling. I'd rather put up with your cousin's glare than stare at those four walls."

"I'm sorry. I know it's easy to go stir-crazy all cooped up here. And don't worry about Sebastian—I'll handle him."

"If he's got a problem with me, I'll be glad to take it up with him outside."

Her mouth went flat. "Spare me the testosterone show, okay?"

"Sure, as soon as your cousin stops looking at me like he wants to kill me."

Lauren leaned in close, her gaze cool and piercing. "My cousin is one of the most dangerous witches you will ever meet. I suggest you give him as wide a berth as you can."

"Or what? He'll kill me? Or is that just what he wants me to believe?"

She said nothing, and he could tell she was choosing her words carefully.

"You really think he'd do something crazy?" he finally asked.

"I don't know what he'd do."

"I think it's time for me to get the hell out of here. I'll take my chances with the assholes who chased you out of San Francisco."

"No," Lauren said, as if that settled the matter. "You will stay here."

"Look babe, I'd love to stick around and see if your cousin will murder me in my sleep, but the truth is, if you and I aren't going to be happening, I've got no reason to stay here."

"The Order will kill you, Carson. They'll torture you and then kill you."

"That doesn't make any sense. Even if they do figure out who I am, torturing or killing me will only bring the police. Because, unlike your elders, my friends and family won't hesitate to go to the authorities. I can't see it happening." He didn't want to sound dismissive of something that Lauren was so serious about, but he honestly didn't believe The Order would track him down. The threat certainly wasn't as strong as the one Sebastian had issued.

"Carson, I'm serious. They will be after you."

In his entire vaguely pointless life, Carson had

never faced actual death. There'd been that car accident in college, but he'd never seen the collision coming. He'd simply woken up in the hospital afterward, in some pain but happily unaware that his car was totaled.

And now, the prospect of death still seemed so far removed from his reality, it was absurd. People didn't get tortured and killed by secret witch-hunting societies in modern-day California.

"And I'm serious. I'm out of here first thing in the morning." He'd try to persuade her to join him and, even if she didn't, he'd figure out some way to lend his support to the witches' fight against The Order.

Lauren sat on the bar stool next to him and a mojito appeared before her. She picked up the glass of clear mint-laced liquid and took a long drink.

"Is this about me? Is it getting too hard to be around me?"

"No, *I'm* getting too hard to be around you." He eyed his own crotch meaningfully, and Lauren's gaze followed his down to his zipper, where his cock was pushing to get out.

She sighed. "Damn it. I'm sorry."

"If we're not going to sleep together, I have to get the hell out of here."

"Is that another ultimatum?"

"Yes."

"If we sleep together, things are going to be more difficult for you."

"How so?"

"You know how—the addiction will become more intense."

"I don't think it gets any more intense than the rock-hard erections I'm walking around with all freaking day."

She shook her head. "It does, I promise. It gets worse."

"So let me take the risk."

She closed her eyes, and he admired the thick black lashes resting against her cheeks. She was exquisite in a way few women were. Not so much because of some outlandish beauty, but because she looked as rare as she was, like some bird you might only spot once in your lifetime and spend the rest of your life craving the sight of again.

He knew what craving Lauren felt like. He'd spent the weeks after Vegas almost in a cold sweat with wanting her again. His dreams had been filled with the erotic sensation of sliding into her, feeling her clench around him. Her scent, her taste, her touch had haunted his days until he'd have given everything he owned to have sex with her just one more time.

So, yeah. He knew the risk in sleeping with a witch. He knew and he still didn't care about the consequences.

When she opened her eyes again, she nodded. "You're sure you want to take that risk?"

"Yeah."

"You'll stay here with me as long as I ask you to?"

"Yeah," he lied. Even with Lauren's body to distract him, he wasn't sure how long he could tolerate her creepy cousin, but he would stay as long as it made sense to do so.

Despite his pressing urge to get the hell out of here, he was beginning to realize he didn't have much to go back to. Something about being with Lauren made his life in San Francisco feel empty and pointless. She had a cause she was personally committed to. Even the work she did as a scientific researcher had purpose and meaning. What did he do? Come up with campaigns to persuade people to part with their hard-earned cash for crap they didn't need or want. Some purpose.

Her gaze turned dark, and he could see a desire in her eyes as clear as what he felt in himself. So she had it bad, too. All thoughts of life purposes fled as he relished getting her naked again. She might have thought avoiding sexual contact was in his best interest, but he knew differently. The only thing he needed was her—over and over until his lust was gone, addiction or no addiction.

And having spent a few years in college dedicated to the pursuit of getting high, he knew what it meant to be addicted. He was the kind of guy who knew how to embrace excess.

And he knew how to go too far.

LAUREN KNEW IT WOULD BE extremely difficult for Carson.

But when faced with the choice—give him a

brutal addiction, or let him walk into the hands of killers—what could she do?

And to make the choice even more obvious, she wanted him as badly as he wanted her.

When she was near Carson, she could barely resist touching him, tasting him, clinging to him and devouring him. She had not felt this way about a man before—not quite in this way. Not quite so desperate.

"Come back to the room," she said, and she led him away.

She didn't dare touch him where Sebastian might see. There was always the risk that Sebastian, with his all-seeing talent, might spy them anyway. If he did, there would be some kind of hell to pay.

But with this situation, no matter how they looked at it, there was going to be hell to pay.

As soon as they were behind the closed door of the room, she pulled Carson to her and kissed him with the absolute yearning she'd been feeling for days.

His tongue plunged into her mouth, caressed hers, as he moaned and roamed his hands over her body. Lauren pressed him against the door and unfastened his pants, found his cock beneath his boxers, grasped it through the thin fabric.

"Damn," he whispered. "I've missed you."

He dipped his head down and bit her neck, licked her shoulder, pushed her breasts up and kissed the tops of them. Then he turned her and pinned her against the door where he had been a moment before.

Lauren closed her eyes and concentrated on the feel of his hands and mouth against her. She'd craved this sensation for so long and now she reveled in it. He tugged at her skirt, baring her thighs to the cool air, an exquisite contrast to the heat consuming her. Without warning, he dropped to his knees, and pulled her panties down. For a few moments he just looked at her, his eyes feasting on her with such intent her insides contracted with sharp longing. She wanted to spread her legs wider, tempt him with even more of her flesh. Finally she could feel his hands moving up her thighs, and his fingertips scarcely touching her pussy, teasing her.

She gasped and squirmed closer, chasing those elusive fingers.

And then his lips and his tongue were there, caressing her, stroking her. Warm liquid sensation. Hot tingling pleasure. Heaven.

Lauren leaned against the door and opened herself to him, her breath quickening. He held her hips as he licked and sucked at her clit, torturing her and edging her closer to the brink of orgasm with every second that passed.

It had been too long for her. She hadn't taken a lover since she'd been with Carson three months earlier. Three long months of denial, of wanting him but thinking she'd never have him again. To have that hunger satisfied now was nearly more than her senses could take.

"Stop," she whispered, not wanting to come too soon, feeling herself getting close.

"Mmm," he moaned as he continued to pleasure her.

"No," she laughed, trying to squirm away but failing. "I want this to last longer than a minute."

He stopped and looked up at her. "Trust me, this will last all night if I have any say in the matter."

She sighed and decided it was time to take control of the situation. Lauren lifted her foot up and pressed the stiletto heel of her sandal against his throat. "Don't make me get rough with you."

His eyes locked on to her sex, revealed so clearly in this position, and she almost came from the erotic expression on his face. "You'd really stab me with your shoe?"

"Would it turn you on?"

"Maybe."

"Then maybe I would."

His gaze traveled up her torso to her face. "I dare you."

Instead, she kicked him gently, just enough to make him lose his balance and fall backward. A moment later, she was on top of him on the floor.

"Don't take it personally," she said as she hovered a few inches from his lips. "I don't want to come so fast."

"I'll make you come at least a dozen times. You know me."

"I know me, too. I want to take it slow. This is dangerous stuff, this addictive sex, you know."

"Seems like everything in my life is dangerous all of a sudden," he whispered.

His gaze half-lidded, he looked drunk, and she didn't know if it was from the whiskey he'd been drinking in the bar, or from her, or both. She'd guess both.

Lauren tugged off her clothes, and straddled Carson again wearing nothing but her heels. Being naked while he remained clothed with only his pants undone should have made her feel overexposed. Instead, she felt the thrill of power and control as his gaze roamed her assets and his hands slid over her body. She leaned down and kissed him long and deep as he grasped her breasts and tugged at her nipples, and that tugging went all the way to her core. She moaned into his mouth, then rocked her hips against his, stroking her sex along his hard cock, but not allowing him in.

"I want inside you," he said.

"You have protection?"

He pulled his wallet out of his back pocket, and Lauren took the packet from him, tore it open with her teeth and took out the condom. She sheathed him, and mounted him in one smooth thrust of her hips.

Having him buried deep inside her, she thought, should have relieved a bit of her craving. Instead it coiled tighter, made her feel more desperate, more needy. She began riding him at an urgent pace, her gaze locked with his as he held tight to her waist and thrust in time with her. He looked as desperate as she felt.

"Don't stop," he gasped. "Don't ever stop."

She couldn't have if she'd wanted to.

She watched his face rapt with pleasure, savored the feel of him bringing her closer and closer to orgasm, and she knew they'd be here all night, satisfying their cravings, making up for lost time.

She wanted to memorize every inch of him, commit him fully to memory and live right here in this moment for as long as she could.

She rocked faster against him, her body tensing as she watched his own body tense.

And as she felt him reach orgasm, she gave in to the sensation, as well, crying out at the jolts of pleasure that shot through her. It went on until the intensity was almost too much to bear, and then it subsided, leaving her spent.

Lauren collapsed, gasping, on the floor, her skin damp with sweat and her body tingling. Carson stretched out long beside her, and pulled her leg over his hip.

"It's been too long since we've done that," he said, looking even more drunk now but sounding completely sober, if a little breathless still.

"Yeah." She stretched, closed her eyes and inhaled his scent.

And at the same time it had been not nearly long enough, because their absence from each other's bed had not cured Carson of his need for her. Next time they parted ways, it would be much, much more difficult for him. And maybe for her, too, given how well their bodies worked together and how powerful their chemistry was.

She winced at the thought of what he would go through, the physical and emotional withdrawal, the lifelong disappointment of never feeling such pleasure again. The weight of guilt settled in her stomach, now that she was satisfied enough to think more clearly.

"I'm sorry," she said. "I shouldn't have done that to you."

He laughed. "Oh yes you should have. And you should have done it sooner, so what the hell are you apologizing for?"

"I just meant, it will feel worse when we're apart again."

"You're already planning our breakup? Why don't we stick around for a while and start driving each other crazy before we start thinking about splitting up?"

Because she would be dead soon—her vision dictated it. But she would not tell him that. Not yet.

"Under normal circumstances, sure, that makes perfect sense. But in case you haven't noticed, we are enduring the most abnormal of circumstances."

"Oh right," he said, mock-surprised. "You're a *witch,* and I'm supposed to get all addicted to you because I'll never have sex even remotely as good as this again in my life."

"Don't be a smart-ass. You know how you felt after Las Vegas. Do you really want to endure that feeling times ten or twenty? Or worse?"

"I can't even imagine."

"I've been through it with someone once before."

"And what? He went insane and jumped off the Golden Gate Bridge because he couldn't have sex with you anymore?"

"Something like that."

She didn't want to explain the whole story. She'd only been nineteen, and she hadn't quite understood the gravity of her power over humans yet.

But he persisted. "Tell me what happened."

"I had a mortal lover my freshman year of college. We dated for about six months until my mother caught wind of what I was doing and told me she'd stop paying my tuition to Stanford if I continued."

"So you broke up with him then?"

"No, actually, I dropped out of college for the rest of the semester and messed around with the guy for a while longer."

"And where's the part about him going crazy when he loses you?"

"He dropped out of school, too. But we eventually burned out on the relationship because it was too intense. I broke up with him, and it was a downward spiral for him after that. I feel like I ruined his life."

Lauren didn't think about Kyle often, and she didn't tell people about him. He'd been this disastrous event in her life that she'd carefully skirted for years—for so long that talking about it now seemed surreal, as if she was recounting something that hadn't really happened.

"You ever hear from him anymore?"

"No. A few months after we broke up, he tried to commit suicide. And after that, he joined a 12-step program for sex addicts, and that was the last I ever heard about him. I'm not proud of the fact that I nearly ruined his life."

"So, these elders you mentioned—they forbid you from ever having sex with mortals? What happens if they find out what you're doing with me?"

"They could banish me from the clan, or have me killed."

"What?" Carson sat up on his elbow and stared hard at her. "Killed? For having sex?"

Lauren shrugged. "They're hard-asses. What can I say?"

"Can't they get put in prison or something for killing people?"

"Witches have had centuries of practice at hiding things. The police are the least of our worries."

"I guess so, if you have to worry about your own family killing you."

"Let's don't think about that, okay? It's a worst-case scenario."

Carson sighed, but said nothing more.

Lauren slid her hand across Carson's belly, lifting his shirt in the process, and admired the contrast of their skin colors, hers pale with the slightest pink undertones, and his light golden brown. "Where do you get so much sun living in the city?"

"I go out hiking and biking a lot on the weekends. Mostly trails in Marin where it's sunnier."

"Ah. Must be a good stress reliever after doing the daily grind all week."

"Yeah, it is. I try to get as far from the job mentally as I can on the weekends."

"I've watched Macy survive that world all these years, and I don't know how you guys do it. I think it would kill me."

"Your job can't be all that low-stress. Medical research is pretty competitive, isn't it?"

Lauren shrugged. "Not in the same way."

"How'd you ever decide to do a study on whether sex makes people dumber? I mean, isn't that kind of a no-brainer?"

She smiled and traced her finger along the little trail of hair that led down toward his cock fully exposed now with his pants down around his ankles. "I had a vision, actually."

"A vision of what? People doing stupid things after orgasms? Putting their shoes on the wrong feet and stuff?"

"No, actually, it all started with the side effects I noticed my lovers experiencing."

"You mean guys were acting like dumb-asses over you? That shouldn't come as any surprise."

"I thought it was a phenomenon worth exploring, anyway, and as I was thinking about it one day, I had a vision that the results of the study would be groundbreaking news. So I got started with it."

"It just seems like such an obvious thing. Do we really need a study to prove it?"

"That's what science is for—to explain the processes that make our world work."

"I guess," Carson muttered and pulled her closer. "Next time, could you do a study about how many orgasms it's possible to achieve in one day?"

"I think we're well on our way to finding the answer to that question. Besides, there isn't going to be any *next time* for me as far as my work goes."

"Oh right. I guess you can't just get a job as a scientist somewhere else?"

She shook her head. "I pretty much have to get myself a new identity now."

"Wow, that really sucks. Won't you miss your old life?"

"Of course I will, but it's not like I have a choice in the matter."

One thing Lauren had learned to accept along with having the gift of prescience—there were far fewer choices in life than anyone ever liked to believe there were.

She closed her eyes and allowed her body to drift toward sleep. Savoring this moment, right now, was the only choice she was sure she could make.

9

LAUREN SAT ON THE EDGE of Sebastian's desk and watched as he scrolled through image after image of suspected Order operatives. She had some shaky memory of the men she'd seen in the vision outside her door, and Sebastian wanted her to point out if any of the men in his database looked like the ones she'd seen that night.

So far, no luck.

"Where is the mortal?" Sebastian asked.

"Carson. His name is Carson. He's probably sitting in the room, bored out of his mind. I don't think he's going to be able to stay here much longer."

"He's lucky I haven't kicked his ass out into the street."

"I don't think he sees it that way. And if you kick him out, I'll leave, too."

He continued to scroll through photos and sketches, and Lauren thought she recognized a sketch that popped up on the screen. "Stop," she said. "That one." She stared at it, trying to recall the image that had come to her before.

One of the men had been tall, in his forties maybe,

with short dark hair and a receding hairline—nearly bald on top. She remembered his eyes best, which were cold and blue.

"He looks familiar?"

"Yes, maybe…" She studied the drawing, but it was impossible to tell if the eyes were the same in the black-and-white sketch. "We don't have a color version of this?"

Sebastian shook his head. "No, and no information on this guy, either, other than that he was heard speaking Czech."

"That matches what I heard in my vision, too. I think that's one of the men."

"Let's keep looking and see if you recognize the other one." He continued to scroll.

"What happens if we figure out who these guys are?"

"Then I will make a special point to track them down and kill them myself."

"Sebastian…" She hated hearing her cousin talk that way.

"You know the uprising can't happen without blood being shed."

"I guess I never thought of it that way. I'd hoped there would be a public outcry from the mortal community against our persecution."

He cast a scornful glance at her. "Don't be naive."

She blinked. Sebastian never talked to her that way before. He'd always been kind to her. He'd always made her feel loved.

"What's happened to you?" she whispered.

She was looking at him now, instead of the photos. She wasn't sure she wanted to identify the men, if it meant her cousin's hands getting soiled with more blood.

He leaned back in his chair and regarded her wearily. "Maybe I sold my soul," he said. "Or maybe I never had one in the first place."

"You had me fooled," she said. "The Sebastian I know has both a heart and a soul."

"You had me fooled, too, cousin. I never thought I'd see the day when you were more loyal to a mortal than you are to me."

She reached out and took his hand, and she looked him in the eye, hoping to reach that place she used to know so well. "It's not about loyalty. It's about doing what's right. I love you, but I have a duty to protect Carson. It's my fault he's in this mess."

"You're going to have to lose that moral conscience if you want the uprising to succeed," he said.

"No, you're wrong. We can't have our freedom at any cost. We have to achieve it justly, or not at all. Otherwise we're simply a version of The Order."

"Is it just that we have to live in hiding, in fear of persecution?"

"Wasn't it Gandhi who said 'An eye for an eye makes the whole world blind'?"

"Spare me the bumper sticker philosophy, Lauren. This is the real world, where we will die if we aren't careful."

They stared at each other, neither willing to back down. An awful feeling settled in Lauren's gut. Was she being naive? She'd never considered the real cost of their freedom. She'd never made herself look hard at that problem, and she'd never asked herself before if she could live with the answer.

For the first time she could remember, she wished she'd never had a vision of an uprising, or a victory, or a sense that they should have ever strayed from the elders' rules.

She suddenly longed for her old life, which was so simple by comparison—her old life, where she knew all the rules. Now it appeared they had to make each rule up as they went along, and she wasn't sure she was up for the task.

LARS DETESTED Los Angeles, but he held a special distaste for West Hollywood. As he and Noam walked the streets of the neighborhood that probably held more witches than any other place on Earth, he could not help but look at every face and try to sense if they were mortal or witch.

And the more beautiful the face, the more suspicious he was about their true identity. It was a cruel joke that witches were more physically beautiful than mortal women, as if their physical appearances were designed to fool and distract normal men.

"You want to stop looking for a while and get some lunch?" Noam asked, glancing at his watch. "It's getting to be that time."

"I saw a sandwich place down the block. We can go there."

They headed in the direction of the deli, and five minutes later, they had each ordered lunch and were sitting at a table waiting for their food.

"Two days and no luck. What do you think that means?" Noam asked.

He was too young and impatient. He would have to learn that the hunt never ended, so there was never a need to be in a hurry.

"I think it means we haven't found Lauren Parish yet."

"What if she's not here?"

"It's like always—if we have enough patience, we'll find what we seek."

Noam's gaze followed a thin, beautiful blonde along the sidewalk as they stared out the window. "You ever slept with a witch?" he asked.

Lars did not know how to answer. While it was officially forbidden for a member of The Order to have sexual relations with witches, it was also commonly accepted that many among them took liberties with their captives before they killed them.

He was torn between wanting to warn the boy about his firsthand experiences with the addiction that came along with having sex with a witch, and wanting to brag that he had indeed taken some of the most beautiful women in the world before killing them.

He chose his words with care. "I'm sure you've

heard rumors of the pleasures that come with taking a witch."

Noam nodded. "Sure. It's all the trainees talk about almost."

"It's been a long time since I've been a trainee. In my time, we didn't dare discuss such things out in the open."

"I guess we've gotten bolder over the years."

"Once you've had a witch, mortal women will feel inadequate to you," Lars warned.

Noam made a whistling sound and shook his head seemingly in appreciation. "I can't wait."

"Shh. Don't say such things so boldly."

"Hell, nobody around here even knows what we're talking about," the kid said, now in his native Czech.

Lars responded in Czech, as well, to be safe. "It's a dangerous addiction, worse than any drug."

"So you have had sex with witches?"

"Many times."

And now he could not even make love to mortal women. His cock wouldn't even get hard for them. It was shameful to admit, but true.

"Then you can't go around telling me not to do it."

"I can at least warn you that you will regret it," Lars said, but he knew the lure was too great.

It was the shameful secret of The Order, that many of its members were addicts. Some had even dared in the past to hold their witch concubines hostage so that they could continue to enjoy the physical pleasures of them. But that had proven too dangerous, and now, as far as Lars knew, the policy was to kill every witch captive.

Their sandwiches arrived, and they went silent as they ate. Then Noam broke the silence with, "What's so great about it? How do they make you get addicted?"

"It's impossible to describe until you experience it. I think that's why so many of us are unable to resist the temptation, and why some of us have died trying to have that pleasure."

"Damn," Noam muttered. "Pussy worth dying for…"

His time would come soon enough. Lars would let him have his way with Lauren Parish if he so desired—after Lars was through with her of course.

"I've heard some of the prostitutes here are really witches," Noam said. "You think we could, you know, check it out?"

"I don't want to waste time with such pursuits."

"Couldn't we consider it another way of finding witches? You know, if the sex is that great, then they must be a witch?"

Lars sighed. "Maybe tonight, if we have no luck this afternoon."

"Hey," Noam said, pointing at a man across the street. "Is that the guy we saw on the camera from her apartment?"

Lars stared at the man, then withdrew from his

chest pocket a photo that they'd produced from the video footage. The man on the sidewalk wore a baseball cap, dark glasses and had the start of a beard, but he had the same brown hair and the same bone structure as the man from the video.

"Let's check him out," he said coolly, and they stood quickly and left the deli. From the opposite sidewalk they followed the man as he headed west, and when he made a left at the next corner and disappeared out of sight, they started across the street. But traffic was heavy, and Lars noticed too late the red Mercedes coming toward them.

The car screeched to a stop, but not before it bumped against Noam and sent him sprawling. Lars's first instinct was to leave the kid behind and run after the man. But when he looked down and saw that Noam wasn't getting right up, he paused.

The kid was his responsibility, and one rule he would never violate was abandoning his apprentice. He knelt beside the kid, who was wincing as he tried to bend his leg. "Are you okay?"

"Yeah, I think so," he said as he grasped his knee. "Just a little scraped up."

"Let me help you up and let's make sure you can walk."

The driver of the Mercedes, a woman in her fifties, looked horrified as she got out of the car.

"Don't worry, ma'am," Lars called out. "He's fine."

The last thing they needed was filing a police

report or making a trip to the hospital. Lars knew how to splint a leg himself, if worse came to worst.

"Come on," he said to Noam as he stood up. "You steady on your feet?"

He nodded.

"If we hurry, we might still catch up to the guy."

Noam took a few tentative steps, dusted off his pants, and said, "I'm fine."

The two men crossed the intersection and broke into a jog as they hit the sidewalk again. Around the corner, the man they'd spotted earlier was nearly a block away now, and they ran to catch up, slowing down only as they came close enough to draw attention from him.

On the next block, he paused at a store window and eyed some lingerie on a mannequin, then continued on.

"I'll grab his wallet if I can, and you keep following him to see where he goes," Lars whispered to Noam.

He nodded his agreement, and then hung back as Lars hurried ahead. He pretended to bump into the man, and as he'd practiced hundreds of times, he slid his fingers quickly into the rear pocket and withdrew the wallet in one fluid movement.

"I'm sorry," he said as he passed by, trying not to make eye contact.

Lars tucked the wallet into his pants and continued on. When he'd reached the safety of their van, he sat in the driver's seat and inspected the contents of the wallet. The driver's license said the man's name was Carson McCullen, and his home address was in San Francisco.

They had found the man they were looking for, and they were one step closer to Lauren Parish.

Fifteen minutes later, Noam returned to the van.

"Where did he go?" Lars asked.

Noam looked sheepish. "I guess my leg wasn't as fine as I thought it was. My knee gave out and I had to stop and let it rest for a minute. I lost him."

"Damn it! He's the man from the video. He lives in San Francisco. You just ruined our freaking chance of grabbing the witch today."

"Well, why the hell did you leave me alone?"

"I thought you could handle it," Lars said, tossing the wallet at the kid.

But the truth was, he'd been careless. No more. From now on, he would leave no stone unturned, and he would not leave the job of a professional to a mere baby.

CARSON HAD SPENT five solid days indoors, and he had been going stir-crazy. He was an outdoor kind of guy, and far as he could remember, this was the first time in his life he'd spent this much time inside.

Lauren was a pretty damn good reason to stay indoors, but when she was busy conspiring with her cousin Sebastian, it left Carson bored as hell. He hadn't seen any harm in going out for a quick walk around the neighborhood, especially when he'd never even *seen* the neighborhood before—and the sunshine and fresh air had been well worth what had seemed like a small risk. However, he knew he was in big trouble when he saw Lauren's face upon arriving back in the hotel room.

"What the hell did you do?" she said coldly.

"I just wanted to go for a walk. I'm so damn sick of being stuck in this place, I couldn't stand it anymore."

Her eyes widened. "You went for a walk. In broad daylight."

"Last time I checked it wasn't a crime." He took off the stupid hat and sunglasses that had been included in the parcel of clothes Sebastian had had delivered for him, and tossed them on the dresser. "At least I wore a disguise."

"Oh yeah, that hat and glasses transformed you into an entirely different person."

"Look, I wanted to experience normal life for a half hour. I'm getting a little tired of being locked up in freak world, where everyone but me has at least one tattoo and a supernatural power."

"How about talking to me? Do you realize what you've done?"

"I went out and enjoyed the sunshine. I saw some people who aren't witches. It felt good. I'm not so stir-crazy now. Big freaking deal."

"It is a big deal. You have no goddamn idea."

"You know, you ripped me out of my everyday life, took me away from my job and my friends and told me there was this whole underground world I didn't know about and now I have to live in it. And you expect me to just sign up for the whole damn vacation to hell package without a second thought?"

She glared at him and said nothing, her arms crossed over her chest.

He flopped onto the bed and sighed, feeling guilty now. "I'm sorry, Lauren. I'm not used to being inside all the time. I'm the outdoorsy type. I need fresh air regularly or I start going insane."

"So go up on the rooftop deck! Don't go out walking around West Hollywood when we've got people who are hunting us down!"

She slammed her fist against the wall for emphasis, then winced at the pain of it.

"Don't you think maybe you're being a wee bit paranoid? There are thousands of people on the street out there, and we're hundreds of miles south of where you last came in contact with the witch hunters."

"I told you, there are rumors that The Order has a network of people here now because they've figured out that witches gravitate to this area. Witches have been disappearing recently."

The guilt twinged stronger. He hadn't intended to put Lauren in danger.

"I'm really sorry," Carson said. "I won't do it again. I promise to follow all the rules from now on."

"Don't you dare let Sebastian know you went out, or he'll be furious. I'll have to tell him…" She appeared to be thinking. "This is bad," she said, running her hand over her face.

Carson resisted rolling his eyes. He was getting the slightest bit tired of having to live under Sebastian's rule, but he said nothing because he was responsible for this particular incident.

"Aren't you maybe overreacting a little? Do you really even need to tell Sebastian?"

"I'm going to have to tell everyone, damn it! The whole place is going to have to be put on alert, with heightened security."

"Shit," he muttered.

"Knowing Sebastian, he won't let anyone out of the building for the next month after he hears this."

"I didn't realize how big a deal it would be."

"Did anything strange happen while you were out?"

"Not a thing," Carson said, but at that moment he noticed the lack of an uncomfortable lump in his rear pocket that was normally created by his wallet.

Then he recalled the man who'd bumped into him. He reached around and felt his pocket, and realized nothing was there.

Damn it. He kept his expression neutral, not sure if it was worth alarming Lauren over.

"What are you doing?" she asked.

"Just looking for the package of gum I bought while I was out. Guess I dropped it."

No, there was no sense in worrying her. She was already on edge about every little thing, and maybe he'd left his wallet somewhere in the room. Or maybe it had fallen out here in the hotel. Yeah, and maybe little elves had come and taken it away.

He had to be sure his wallet was really stolen, though, before he risked freaking Lauren out. Hearing that he'd lost it to a pickpocket might have put her off the deep end.

10

WITH NOTHING ELSE TO DO and no one allowed to so much as breathe in the direction of the outside world now, Carson and Lauren tended to hang out at the club every night, where the other witches displayed varying degrees of hostility about his presence, especially since the leaving-the-hotel incident.

He'd gotten enough scathing looks and disgusted glares to last him a lifetime after Sebastian ordered the entire place to go on lockdown and forbade all witches from setting foot outside. One guy had even attacked Carson in the elevator, slamming him up against the wall and clenching his hand around Carson's neck, but Lauren had stepped in and explained how Carson hadn't understood the gravity of leaving the hotel.

A woman sidled up to the bar next to Carson and waited for the bartender to notice her so she could order a drink. When Carson glanced at her, she smiled wickedly.

"Stupid human," she whispered. "You're lucky to still be alive."

And she was right, apparently. He was. He finally understood that.

How Lauren heard the woman's words over the loud music in the club was beyond Carson, but she had. "Shut the hell up," she said to the woman, who glared at Lauren for a second, then turned and walked away.

Lauren took Carson's hand and tugged him toward the dance floor, so he downed the last of his scotch and let her lead the way. In the darkness of the pulsing crowd, she was all he cared about. He could ignore the weird vibes from the witches surrounding them when she was in the room.

He pulled her close right before they reached the dance floor, and said, "You are stunning."

She smiled coyly back at him. "So are you."

He watched her ass in the skimpy white fringed dress she wore. In a sea of dark colors, she stood out like a vision from heaven. And it enticed him all the more that he knew she was anything but.

The way she moved was so natural, so fluid, so full of raw sexuality, that when she found a place for them among the other pulsing bodies and began dancing, there was no point at which her walking had stopped and her dancing started. She turned to him, her hips swaying to the techno-tribal beat of the music, and her gaze was heavy with what he had come to recognize as desire.

For him.

Amazing.

He started dancing with her, against her, their bodies moving in time, and the heat of the bodies all around them immediately drenched him in sweat. Carson ignored the feel of his clothes sticking to his body and let the music entrance him along with Lauren.

She was nothing like he'd originally thought, months ago in Las Vegas. And yet she was. It was as if he was watching her shed the trappings of her buttoned-up life in the real world and let herself become who she really was, here in safety among the witches.

She was his addiction and his cure, all rolled up into one irresistible package.

She leaned in close and asked, "What's wrong? You look distracted."

"Nothing," he lied. "I guess I won't ever get used to being the lone mortal in the room."

"Don't worry," she said into his ear, barely audible over the music. "They'll get over it."

"I don't belong here," he said.

"I'll decide that. You belong here as long as I'm protecting you."

He bristled at the thought, but said nothing. He had his male pride, but he knew better than to go around puffing it up in front of a woman like Lauren. The truth was, he wanted to be protecting her, not the other way around. He wanted to kill any bastard that would dare harm her, but he didn't exactly feel equipped yet to navigate the world of witches and witch hunters effectively.

After all, it was a world he hadn't even known existed most of his life.

But the fact remained that he would do anything he could to keep Lauren safe. He would learn all about her world if it meant he could somehow help her.

He placed his hands possessively on Lauren's hips as she danced, and he let his mind drift to more base thoughts. Of their bodies moving together not here on the dance floor, but somewhere more private. Somewhere free of these goddamn stifling clothes.

She pressed herself against him and felt his erection. Her gaze dropped for a moment to his crotch, then traveled up again to meet his. "You want to get out of here?"

"We just got here."

"It's hot as hell in here," she said. "Come with me. I know someplace we can cool off."

Five minutes later, they were away from the deafening dance music and the stifling crowd of witches. They'd gone up four flights of stairs, through a door marked Employees Only, and out onto a rooftop deck with an utterly amazing view of the city.

"Wow," Carson said as he took in the lights, the night sky and the Hollywood sign on the distant hillside.

"Yeah. Welcome to my favorite place in Hollywood. Sebastian doesn't tell anyone about it. It's his own place to escape from all his responsibilities."

"Will he mind us being here?"

"No, I'm one of the few people he'll let come up

here any time. Besides, he's busy with the club tonight. He won't even know we're here."

Carson surveyed the deck. Right in the middle of it was an outdoor fireplace, and a bed with an outdoor canopy over it. "I guess we know what goes on up here, huh?"

Lauren shrugged and headed for the fireplace, which was a minimalist glass cube with a small fire pit in bottom. A flick of a switch brought flames to life. Instant fire.

"Cool," he said.

"I doubt Sebastian brings women up here," she said. "But he does sleep up here sometimes. He likes the outdoor air."

"What? Your cousin's celibate or something?"

"No, but he's very private, and he doesn't let many people get close to him. It's part of his way of protecting the witch clan. To be a protector, he has to be inaccessible, I guess."

"To make sure the wrong person doesn't get too close to him?"

"Something like that."

"Have any of those witch hunter guys ever infiltrated this place?"

"Yes," she said, but he heard some hesitation in her voice.

"What happened?"

"They were found out," she answered, and he had a sense that he shouldn't ask any more questions about the subject.

He came up behind Lauren and pushed the thick curtain of her dark hair aside, then kissed the tattoo on her neck. "Does this mean something?" he asked, tracing the design with his finger.

"It's Celtic. I can't tell you what it means, but it represents the essence of my power, if that makes any sense."

"It doesn't, but I'll take your word for it," he teased, then kissed her there again, this time letting his lips linger.

His hands found their way up her rib cage to the heavy curves of her breasts, and he massaged them slowly, his cock aching as he felt her nipples harden.

His addiction to her was growing by the day, by the hour, by the minute, and he was helpless to control it. When he thought of living a day without making love to Lauren, his stomach went sour.

In the firelight, her tattoo looked especially luminous, as if it were somehow alive separate from her. He thought of the raven tattoo on Sebastian's arm, and he didn't doubt for a moment their supernatural powers.

"What happens if a mortal falls in love with a witch?" he asked.

Lauren turned to him, gazing at him with dark, unfathomable eyes. Even the firelight didn't lighten them. "I don't know," she said.

"Is it like selling your soul to the devil?"

"Witches aren't evil," she said.

"I know that, I just meant—"

"None of the stereotypes you've ever heard are true. We're not the brides of Satan. We don't ride broomsticks or wear pointy hats, and we don't go around stirring cauldrons or casting spells."

"I'm sorry, I didn't mean to insult you."

"It's okay. I get touchy about the subject."

"Where do you think all those stereotypes came from?"

"I'm sure some of my ancestors did some of that stuff. I mean, people used to cook in cauldrons. And both witches and nonwitches alike attempt to practice black magic. It doesn't have anything to do with being a witch, though."

"So all the myths were invented by people who were afraid of witches."

"Perhaps. Over the centuries, The Order had plenty to do with demonizing witches and making the public afraid of us."

"Why?"

"Like you said before, it's a form of racism, just like Hitler attempting to eradicate the Jews or the Turks massacring the Armenians or the KKK trying to scare blacks out of the South."

"Yeah, I see what you mean."

"Our battle is a lot more ancient than that. It's been going on since before recorded history, as far as we know."

"Amazing that it's been kept secret all this time."

"It hasn't always been. There were times in history when witch hunting was more acknowledged by the public, the Salem Witch Trials being the most recent example. But The Order has managed to keep themselves mostly a secret from the world. That's their talent—even better than us—that they know how to stay hidden."

"Maybe the key to stopping them is finding a way to make their actions public."

"But that would mean making ourselves public, as well. It's a tricky thing. We have to choose our time."

"You seem to have some idea when that time is."

"Not exactly, but I know someday that things will change for the better. Maybe not when I'm around to witness it, but someday."

A chill went up Carson's spine at her words. "Of course you'll be around to witness it. Don't sound so doom and gloom."

He cupped her chin in his hand and tilted it up so she had to look him in the eye, but she said nothing. She simply stared at him, her gaze still unknowable to him, filled with something like sadness.

"What is it? Have you had some vision about yourself?"

Her lips parted as if to speak, but she said nothing.

"You have, haven't you?"

She smiled, but it looked forced. "What I'm having a vision of right now is you and me on that bed, naked. Think you can accommodate me?"

"Are you trying to bewitch me to distract me from the subject?"

"Call me wicked," she said, smiling still. "I won't deny it."

She slid her hand down his belly, and her fingers traced the head of his cock through his pants. He expelled a gush of air as she gripped him and massaged gently.

"You're wicked," he said. "And I love it."

She unzipped his fly and pushed him until he was at the edge of the bed, then sitting on it. She took his dick out of his boxers and knelt between his legs. He was aching as he watched her long, delicate fingers encircle him.

Then she dipped her head and took him into her mouth, and he felt a jolt of satisfaction as real as if he'd just taken a hit of the world's most powerful drug. Perhaps he had.

She ran her tongue up and down the length of him as he watched her, disarmed by her beauty and her skill with his body. He didn't think, for as long as she was in his life, he'd ever stop being amazed at what it was like to be with her. Perhaps that was the addiction talking, but one thing he knew about this addiction— the pleasure was the most real thing he could imagine.

There was nothing artificial about it.

She took him all the way into her mouth again, and he moaned at the sensation of it, closing his eyes and letting the whole experience become about the feel of her mouth on his dick. As she worked his body, he felt the pressure building within himself, and he had to find the willpower to stop her. But she knew his body too well—right before he reached the edge of orgasm, she stopped and smiled sinfully up at him.

"You didn't think I'd let you have all your fun now, did you?" she whispered, barely audible above the street sounds and the distant bass of the club music below.

"I was going to stop you," he said, smiling, but he wasn't sure he could have summoned the strength.

He tugged her up from the deck, found a condom in his wallet and put it on as she crawled onto the bed next to him.

Then she was kissing him with an eroticism that almost took him back to that edge. She straddled him, her dress bunched up around her waist, and the sight and feel of her pussy on him was too much pleasure to bear. He lay back, gasping raggedly, as she began riding him. His hands on her waist, he didn't even have the strength to guide her.

He was simply helpless under her spell.

LAUREN WAS BEGINNING to suspect there was no such thing as a single orgasm with Carson. She'd already come once, only minutes after they'd started making love. She hadn't exactly intended to, but the sensation of his body inside her, along with the night air, and the firelight, pushed her over the sensory edge into a realm of pleasure she couldn't control.

But now he was lying on top of her, his weight a delicious pressure and he moved inside her, and she felt herself building toward orgasm again. It was rare that she could come in the good old missionary position, but Carson's cock fit her so perfectly, he rubbed all the right places.

"That's it," she gasped into his ear, and then he covered her mouth in a long, desperate kiss.

He was getting close, too. She could feel the tension in his body building, as the thrusting of his hips grew more urgent, and all she could do was wrap her legs around him and hold on. She stared up at the stark white canopy above them, and she imagined she could see stars.

Except there were rarely stars of the celestial variety visible in Hollywood. The smog was too thick, and the city lights too intense. Rather, what she saw was the way Carson made some kind of magic with her body, a magic she wasn't capable of on her own.

She grasped his wide, firm shoulders as he braced himself on his elbows, and with a final few thrusts, he spilled into her, just as her body contracted around his cock in a second orgasm that was more intense than her first. She cried out at the delicious sensation of it, gasping as he gasped.

When she opened her eyes again after the rush had passed, she saw him staring at her, his brow damp with sweat, his gaze softened from pleasure.

He eased himself down and kissed her again, this time slowly, tenderly, his tongue brushing lightly against hers.

"You," he murmured against her lips.

"What about me?" she said when he pulled back.

"I want to stay in this bed forever with you. Think your cousin will mind?"

She smiled. "Likely he will mind. In fact, we'd better get out of here before too long or he'll come up here and find us."

"And then there'll be hell to pay."

"If it were just me, no, but with you, he's a bit touchy."

"I'm not used to being so thoroughly hated."

"Don't take it personally. It's not really about you, anyway."

"He couldn't possibly like the thought of you sleeping with a mortal."

Carson slid off her, pulled off his condom and dropped it over the edge of the bed into a wastebasket next to the nightstand. Then he returned to her side and pulled her tight against him.

"Don't worry about what he would or wouldn't like. My life is my own, and I decide who I do or don't sleep with."

"Do you think he'd do anything violent to enforce that no sex with mortals rule?"

Lauren gazed at his chest, in love with the firm curves of it, the flat brown nipples, the smooth skin. She didn't want to answer his question, but maybe shielding him from the truth wasn't exactly fair.

"Sebastian has changed since I knew him as a

kid. He scares me now. I don't think he'd harm me, but—"

He sat up. "But you think he'll harm me."

"Don't overreact. I'm probably being paranoid. It's sort of an unspoken thing that some of us break the sex with mortals rule and don't talk about it. Because of my history, the consequences could be harsher."

"Isn't death kind of a harsh punishment?"

"It's a stupid, archaic rule, and that's why I don't abide by it. It has its value, at least as far as protecting mortals from addiction and protecting us from any negative consequences of such an addiction. But as far as mating goes, it's wrong to keep us so limited."

He didn't look satisfied.

"Look," she said, "I'm a scientist. I know there isn't any permanent physical harm that can come from us sleeping together. Genetically, at least, if we were going to produce offspring, we'd actually be giving them a strong advantage. So at least in theory it's a good practice."

"Then why do you look worried?"

"I'm not worried," she lied. "The elders are superstitious and old-fashioned. Modern science doesn't mean much to them in the face of ancient traditions and rules."

"Lauren, I couldn't live with myself if something happened to you because of me." His expression had gone deadly serious, and she could see he was speaking from the heart.

"I feel the same about you," she said, but his words kicked her in the stomach.

She thought of her vision, of the two of them on the beach, in danger. He would survive, and she would not. How would he live with that? Maybe she needed to tell him the whole truth.

It was wrong to keep hiding it from him.

Lauren sat up and grabbed her dress from the side of the bed, then tugged it on. When she was covered, she sat on her knees and regarded him seriously.

"Listen, there's something I should tell you. This might sound awful, but I know how my life ends."

He blinked. "What are you talking about?"

"I've had a vision of my own death. It's common to those of us with the gift of prescience. Some gift, huh?"

He shook his head. "Why are you telling me this? Are you saying it happens soon or something?"

She didn't usually talk about her vision. It was, at the very least, a downer, and at worst, a major conversation-killer even among witches. Besides, she didn't like to think about it.

"I'm telling you because you're there when it happens."

"Hell no," he said, scowling now. "I'm not going to stand by and watch you die. Are you crazy? Your vision must be wrong."

She held up a hand to silence him. "Please," she said. "Just listen."

"But…" He was shaking his head in disbelief.

"I know it sounds really shitty, but you have to remember that there are some things in life we have no control over. I wasn't sure whether I should tell you this. It seems almost too cruel to bring up."

"Then why? Your vision must be wrong. Don't you have wrong ones sometimes?"

"Not like this. It's a recurrent vision, and it never changes."

"What happens?" For a moment, he stopped looking and sounding like the brave, strong man he was, and she caught a glimpse of the scared little boy he once might have been.

She looked away, appalled at herself for doing this to him. It wasn't information that anyone deserved to have. The way he looked, it was as if he really cared about her, as if he were here because of something much stronger than an addiction.

It was wrong and cruel for her to hope for that, or encourage it. It would only lead to more pain for him, if he really cared about her.

She looked back at him, and she realized at that moment exactly how big a wall she'd built around herself. She'd tried to keep herself from caring about him because she could never trust that he was with her for anything more than his next fix. And maybe that's really all it was. But the stricken look on his face made her consider that he did actually care about her. Or could care. And maybe she wanted him to.

No, scratch that. She did want him to care. There was no doubt.

He'd scaled her wall, and she had no idea how to get him out of her heart now.

"I shouldn't say any more. I'm sorry for bringing it up," Lauren said and tried to climb off the bed, but Carson grabbed her arm and held her there.

"You can't just drop a bomb like that on me and not give me any details. I need to know what you saw so we can stop it from happening."

"There's something I've learned from having visions," she said. "Fate is strange. There are some elements of it we can change easily, and there are other parts of our fate that no matter how much we try to avoid them, our destiny twists back around and happens anyway."

"That's bullshit. Tell me what's supposed to happen.'"

She was surprised by the roughness in his normally laid-back, no-worries voice. Surprised enough that she finally said it. "We're running on a beach at night, running from someone, and I get shot."

He sighed heavily. "So we simply don't go to the beach. That's not too hard, is it?"

She shook her head. "Remember what I said about fate. It's a tricky thing."

"What makes you think I don't get shot?"

"It's a vision of my death, not yours. You'll escape. I know that much."

"Lauren, I'm not going to stand by and watch you die. There has to be something we can do about this."

"I've been seeing my own death since I was a little kid. It's not exactly a surprise to me anymore."

He was shaking his head, his brow furrowed, looking as if he'd just received some news he couldn't accept.

She felt like scum. Lower than scum. She should not have told him. She hadn't anticipated how awful it would feel to share the news of her death with the person who would witness it.

"I'm leaving then. If you're supposed to die, then I have to get the hell away from you. We can't ever see each other again."

Lauren stared at her own hands, trying to think how to convince him that it was useless to fight this fate, that they might as well enjoy themselves until the end came. But when she looked up at him, she could see that his eyes were full of grief, that he needed to feel as though he was doing something to help her.

"I really do appreciate your concern," she said. "But maybe the very act of your leaving would be what draws us back together and leads to my getting shot. Do you see how that could work?"

There was a sound from the entrance to the rooftop deck, and they both looked over at the same time to see Sebastian standing in the way, staring at them in complete disgust.

"What the hell are you doing?" he said so low Lauren was sure she was the only one who'd heard.

Carson, next to her, was still naked, and she could

see now there was no way Sebastian was going to be okay with a naked mortal on his bed with her. She'd been stupid to take the risk of bringing Carson here.

"I'm sorry, Sebastian," she said. "We shouldn't have come up here."

"No, you shouldn't have."

"I wanted to get some fresh air, and I didn't think you'd mind if we came up here for a bit to escape the nightclub crowd. But then things got out of hand, and—"

She stopped when she realized she was explaining too much, and Sebastian wasn't even looking at her. He was glaring only at Carson now, so that she wasn't even sure her cousin had heard her.

"We'll go," she said.

Then he looked at her with a coldness she'd never seen before. "The mortal will not be leaving here alive."

11

If the mortal would be the witness to Lauren's death, then it was the mortal who had to die first. Then, Sebastian reasoned, his cousin's vision of her death on the beach could not come true. She might never forgive him for killing her lover, but she would get to live out the full length of her life. That mattered more to him than forgiveness.

Sebastian reached into his boot and withdrew the knife from his ankle holster. "Lauren, you have to leave now," he said coolly.

She must have caught the glint of silver metal in the firelight, because she was staring at the knife now. "No," she said. "Sebastian, don't."

His cousin moved so that she was between him and Carson, but it would only take a few quick moves for him to be in position to throw the knife. He only needed one good throw, and the mortal would be as good as dead. A knife in the heart, or the side of the throat, or the eye—three easy spots to bring death. He'd been practicing knife-throwing since childhood, and he'd never met anyone who could match his skill.

"Lauren, move out of the way," Carson said. "This is between me and your cousin."

"Don't be stupid," she said. "You can't sacrifice yourself for me. It's not going to change anything. I'll still die when it's my time."

"I'm not going to let you get killed on my behalf," Carson said, standing up from the bed and crossing his arms in some kind of ridiculous challenge to Sebastian's knife.

"At least your mortal lover has some courage," Sebastian said. "Let him exercise it so he can die like a man."

He caught Lauren's movement from the corner of his eye, and then he realized she was digging something out of her purse. He heard the click of metal against metal.

"I'll shoot if I have to," she said, and he looked over to see she was aiming the same small gun at him that he'd made her take yesterday to protect herself.

"You've got your loyalties confused, cousin," he said, turning his attention back to the mortal.

Carson glanced over at Lauren's gun, apparently dumbfounded. "What the hell are you doing with that?" he said.

"Sebastian gave it to me for occasions like this," she said quietly. And then to Sebastian, she said, "My loyalties lie with the innocent, which you are not."

He laughed, but he didn't think anything was funny. He thought of the way he'd spent his life defending the family, protecting every goddamn witch who had come into his life, and he felt nothing but sad that his dearest cousin would now think of taking him out over a useless mortal.

He could end it right here. He could throw the knife, and save Lauren's life. If she killed him, then at least all the freaking pain would be gone.

"I'd rather die than leave you to the hands of The Order," he said, "So go ahead and shoot me when I throw this. I don't give a damn. You'll be doing me a favor."

Her expression was cool and even, but if he knew her at all, he knew she wasn't so sure of what to do.

"I just want to say one thing," Carson said. "Why don't you both save yourselves some trouble having to dispose of dead bodies. I was about to leave anyway."

Sebastian eyed the naked man who'd just been lounging on his bed. "Yeah, looks like you were on your way right out the door."

"I don't want to see Lauren die any more than you do. I'll do anything I can to keep her from coming to harm."

Out of the blue, he felt a moment's sympathy for the mortal. He was simply a weak, powerless man who'd fallen into Lauren's web. It was, after all, she who should have known better than to be sleeping with a mortal. "I'm listening," he said without lowering the knife.

"I'll leave and never come anywhere near Lauren

again. If I stay away from her, then there's no way she can die on the beach with me, right?"

"Sebastian, you know you need to be alive to help Corinne when the uprising begins. You're a part of that destiny. I don't want to shoot you and hurt the clan's chance for that freedom…but I will if I have to."

He regarded his cousin curiously. "You care about this mortal that much?"

"I do," she whispered.

Sebastian looked at Carson, and he felt a moment's sympathy for Lauren, who now knew what it was like to want someone she couldn't have. Just the way he wanted Maia, and would never have her.

He was silent as he considered the words on the tip of his tongue. Then he dropped his hand with the knife to his side. "Go," he said to Carson. "Before I change my mind."

The mortal eyed him suspiciously, and Lauren didn't put away her gun. She kept it leveled at Sebastian, as Carson gathered his clothes from the floor and dressed. A minute later, he edged past Sebastian, his gaze pinning him with no small amount of hostility. He got credit, at least, for having balls, and for caring enough about Lauren to get the hell away from her.

When Carson had disappeared through the doorway, Lauren finally put away her gun.

"I'm hurt, cousin. You put a mortal above a family alliance."

She looked at him for the first time with pure, unabashed disgust. "I don't know you anymore, Sebastian. I don't know what happened to you."

Then she followed the mortal out the door, and Sebastian stood on his rooftop deck alone, staring listlessly at the fire. After a while, he went to the edge of the bed and sank onto it. The knife slipped from his fingers onto the deck.

He didn't know what had happened to himself, either. Somewhere along the line, he suspected that bearing the weight of the supernatural world on his shoulders had turned him into a broken man.

"DON'T GO YET," Lauren said. "Let's talk about this first."

Carson turned to her, and for the first time, she realized her hands were shaking. Could she have really shot her own cousin, her blood, someone she'd loved for as long as she could remember?

She feared she could have.

"I'm causing nothing but trouble. Knives, guns, visions of death. It's time for me to get the hell out of here and leave you alone."

"No," she said. "First we have to talk."

Carson pulled a phone book out of the desk. "I need to find a rental car place, and then I'll be out of your hair."

"I'm sorry about Sebastian," she said. "I'm not sure I'll ever forgive him for what he almost did."

"He's just trying to protect you," Carson said. "I

can't blame him for that. I'd probably try to kill me, too, if I were in his shoes."

"You men and your goddamn egos. When are you going to realize it's not all about what you want, all the time?"

"What? You think your death will be for the greater good or something? You think I should stand by and watch it happen without trying to stop it?"

Lauren saw the anguish in his eyes and her words caught in her throat. It felt good to know he cared about her so much, so quickly. Perhaps it was only his addiction coloring his feelings, but some part of her wanted very much to believe his emotions meant something more profound.

She was a fool.

"Thank you for caring," she said, "but I do believe my death is part of something bigger. I believe it's the event that galvanizes my sister's energy and begins the uprising." This was the first time she'd articulated the greater significance hidden in her vision.

"If your sister is so powerful, why can't she save you?"

Lauren sat on the edge of the bed, suddenly feeling tired of having to explain the nature of fate. "I wish I could answer that, but maybe you'd just have to know Corinne."

"What does that mean?"

"She's all power and no discipline. Sort of like a loose fire hose when she tries to make anything happen."

"Then how is she supposed to be the leader of this big uprising?"

"She needs something that forces her to grow up and accept her destiny. She's not mature enough. She believes it, but she also thinks it's all a big game, and she's simply the one who wins."

"Can't you just tell her the deal? That you'll die if she doesn't get her act straight?"

"I've considered that, but I know her. She's never had any real responsibility in her life. She's been incredibly sheltered and spoiled, and I know it's going to take something huge to make her accept that she has to grow up."

"Isn't the threat of her own sister dying huge enough?"

"Maybe, but maybe not. I have to accept my vision for what it is. It's not really my job to question it."

"That's bullshit," he said, slamming his hand against the phone book. "I'm leaving, and I don't want you to ever come near me again. Do you understand?"

Lauren shook her head. "You know, if you go back to your old life, the men who were chasing me might find you."

"I guess I'll have to take that risk. I'm not going to give them any information about you, I promise."

"They have awful ways of getting information, and they'll simply kill you if you don't cooperate."

"Then I'll die. I'd much rather do that than stand by on some goddamn beach and watch you die."

"Please, Carson, don't do this."

"Those guys are after you, not me. I don't think you have anything to worry about."

"If you leave, you'll be putting my life in as much danger as you would if you stayed here."

"Your knife-wielding cousin up there isn't going to go for me sticking around here."

She said nothing, because he was right. Most likely, the witch hunters had gotten tired of trying to track down any leads for her in San Francisco. She was being overly paranoid. Probably enough time had passed now that he would be safe to return to the city.

"You can take Macy's car back to her," she said, and her heart sank as she accepted the inevitable.

12

CARSON HAD BEEN ABLE to cancel his credit cards after his wallet was stolen, but now he had only five hundred dollars he'd borrowed from Lauren.

About halfway to San Francisco, he started feeling the symptoms of withdrawal in a big way. His hands shook, his vision went blurry, and he had a craving so deep and intense it was all he could do to keep from turning the car around and driving straight back to L.A., straight back to Lauren.

She hadn't been kidding about the addiction thing.

After their time in Vegas, he hadn't felt this shitty. Yes, he'd experienced some physical side effects of being apart from her—sleepless nights, intense craving, uncontrolled fantasies—but he'd channeled some of that reaction into his obsession over finding her again.

Now, however, he knew it was over. He'd do everything in his power to stay away from her. So not only were his physical reactions more intense because he'd spent more time with her, but also his emotions were suffering from what he suspected, if he examined it closely, was a broken heart.

He was a little surprised he could still drive the car without wrecking it, given his out-of-control body and mind. Sex had most definitely dumbed him down, as Lauren's study had proven it would.

He thought of his lost wallet, of the risk he'd taken in going out on the street, of how sluggish and stupid he felt right now. He really was acting dumber than usual, and it had to be a side effect of all the sex they'd been having.

He couldn't say he hadn't been warned. He only hoped he hadn't lost so much IQ that he was making mistakes he wasn't even aware of.

He drove north on I-5 and tried to remember why he was leaving. He had to stay away from Lauren to save her life. That alone was worth any amount of pain, and he could endure this physical distress if he knew he was preventing her vision from coming to fruition.

The premonition couldn't come true if he wasn't with her. He just had to remember that.

When these awful feelings intensified, and he was tempted to go running back into her arms, he had to remember that he was saving Lauren's life every day he didn't see her again. It seemed a cruel twist of fate, but maybe it was all for the best after all.

Maybe his parents had been right all those years ago in claiming people of different races were set up to face too many problems as a couple. He and Lauren had certainly proven their point.

But that thought only made him furious. No, his parents were asses.

And someday, somehow, he'd find a way to help Lauren aside from staying away from her. As his hands shook, and he struggled to keep his eyes focused on the road ahead, he promised himself he would find a way to protect her if it was the last thing he did.

CARSON POWERED UP the computer on his desk and tried to work up some kind of enthusiastic feeling for being back at work. A look at his e-mail told him he had 1568 new messages waiting for him, and a glance at his intray told him he had enough work backed up now to keep him busy for, oh, say, the next year. So much for Joey Brennan filling in as Creative Director during the past week.

He downed a long drink of his espresso—his second—and set the cup down as he observed his own shaking hands. He was still experiencing the withdrawal symptoms and he was sleeping like shit. His craving for Lauren was so intense he couldn't even imagine how he'd managed to drive away from her.

But he was feeling better than the day before.

He held on to that.

There should have been some kind of satisfaction in being back in his normal life, but Carson felt only blah. He now saw the pointlessness that he'd suspected while in L.A.—his empty apartment, his voice mail full of messages from people he didn't really care about hearing from, his goddamn job.

Carson realized, upon setting foot back in the Bronson and Wade offices, that he absolutely, without-a-doubt, hated his job.

Through his twenties he'd kidded himself with the notion that he was on the fast track, that he had a killer job in a desirable profession and that was all that mattered. He was being creatively challenged, and how many people ever got to say that about their work?

The advertising world had been a perfect setting for letting him fool himself into believing what the rest of the world said about him—that he was a party boy, a spoiled brat, a good-time guy just out for the next thrill and the next hot babe.

Carson, he was now realizing, had ironically fallen for his own spin. He was an ad man. He was supposed to know better than to fall for the slick package, the surface message, or even the subliminal one.

But he had. And now, why was he so surprised to discover the urge to run away from the whole gig, join the Peace Corps, or maybe expatriate to Bali to buy a nice little hut on the beach? He'd forgotten who he even was.

He opened a message from his boss about a major client who wasn't happy with the direction of their campaign, and his eyes glazed over. He didn't give a damn.

Instead of replying, he closed the message, picked up the phone, and dialed Griffin.

A few rings later, Griffin answered with a, "Hey, man, you're alive. It's about time you called me."

"Sorry, it's been a crazy week, to say the least. I'll explain it all later, or at least I'll try," he lied, not sure what he could really even say about Lauren, L.A. or witches without betraying Lauren's trust. At the very least he knew he would never reveal her true identity. He'd have to make up a good tall tale to explain his absence and Lauren's weird behavior the night they'd gone to her apartment—and why the apartment was ransacked for that matter.

"So you hooked up with Lauren, eh?"

"Don't want to kiss and tell, you know," Carson said, embarrassed at the stiffness in his own voice.

It didn't sound like something he'd say. Until recently, he'd been the king of kissing and telling Griffin the *Reader's Digest* version of his sexual exploits.

"Dude, I get it. You're falling hard for her. We pretty much already knew that."

"I didn't call to talk chicks, honestly. I was actually hoping to talk shop."

"What's up at good old Bronson and Wade, anyway?"

"Can't say we're doing all that great without you and Macy. You can rest assured you were valuable members of the company."

"Give me a break. There were probably five hundred equally talented people lined up to take my job."

Carson sighed. "No kidding. I had to interview them all."

"I know, I know. Sorry to have made your job more difficult, man."

"Hey, I should be glad you're gone, right? It means I'm getting the fat paycheck now instead of you." He was trying to sound cheery, but instead, his voice came out flat.

"What's really going on?" Griffin said.

Carson toyed with a pen on his desk, spinning it with his fingers, attempting to ignore the sick feeling in his gut. But finally, he knew he couldn't keep his worry inside any longer. He'd have to spill it and risk sounding like an idiot.

"Do you ever feel like…um…we're selling our souls in this business?"

He braced himself for a verbal assault, but instead Griffin laughed. "We work in advertising. Of course we're selling our souls. Isn't that a given?"

"How do you live with it? Doesn't it ever start to feel shitty?"

"I don't know, man. I guess it's easier for you to feel unsatisfied when you've got your trust fund to fall back on."

"Sorry, dude. It wasn't a fair question."

"I guess I look at it as a way to earn a paycheck. And I'm always up for a creative challenge."

"And you don't mind bending over and taking it in the ass from clients every day," Carson said, then immediately regretted insulting his best friend yet again.

But again, Griffin surprised him by laughing. "Guess not. I mean, sure, it gets to me sometimes. But I don't take the job too seriously. It's not my whole life or anything."

Of course it wasn't, because Griffin had started his own company, putting himself in a situation where he got to make all the decisions and pick and choose clients. And he had Macy, too, who was probably a hell of a lot more fulfilling than any job.

Carson had only begun to get a taste of what it was like to have something besides work define his existence. And he wanted a bigger taste. He wanted to pull up to the table and have a five-course meal that didn't include the advertising world.

"I'm just getting this feeling that I'm living the wrong life or something."

"Give it some time, man. It takes a few days to get back in the workaday groove."

"No, it's bigger than that. I can't be an advertising whore and ever really be happy with my life."

"So what, you're going to become a trust fund hippie? Turn on, tune in and drop out of your day job?"

"I don't know, man. I don't know." ·

"This is going to sound gay, but remember that time we went on that adventure tour of Costa Rica? We were hiking through the jungle and river rafting and diving off cliffs and shit, and right in the middle of it, I looked at you and said I could hardly recognize you?"

"Yeah, I remember." It had been one of the happiest times in his life, living nearly free of the civilized world, away from all the trappings and the success and the expectations. Away from everything that weighed him down in life.

"That's what this conversation is reminding me of. I haven't seen that side of you in a long time."

"I guess I left it in Costa Rica."

"You seemed more like…yourself then. More like a guy at rest in his own skin, not trying to put on an act for anyone."

"I seem like I'm putting on an act?" Carson said, glancing out the door of his office and hoping no one was lurking nearby eavesdropping on this ridiculously heartfelt conversation. Carson didn't do heartfelt on the job, or anywhere outside of bed.

"Not exactly. I think it's only something I notice because I've seen that other side of you. I've seen the wild, untamed Carson."

"Jungle Boogie Carson?"

"Yeah, man. I think maybe you belong in the jungle, and not the urban one, if you know what I mean."

"Maybe I *am* putting on an act. Or I have been, all these years. That's what scares me most. I started believing my own act."

"It's a good act. I think everyone believes you're the slick, easygoing, good-time guy you make yourself out to be."

"I'm thinking about quitting my job," Carson blurted out, surprised to hear the words spoken aloud himself.

"Yeah, well, I can't say I'd blame you for a second, since I did it myself."

"I just don't know what the hell I want to do."

"At the risk of sounding like a motivational speaker, sometimes you have to make the leap, and then the answer presents itself."

Carson felt a wisecrack on the tip of his tongue, but he held it back. Maybe Griffin was right. Maybe he just needed to leap, without knowing what was at the bottom of the cliff. He thought of Lauren and her quest to live by her own rules, and he realized she'd inspired him. She'd made him want to create some rules of his own.

"You went away for a week and came back sounding like a different person," Griffin said. "What the hell happened to you on that trip, anyway?"

Carson stopped spinning the pen and noticed the Web site advertised on the side of it. Yet another stinking advertisement. His whole life had become messages designed to sell things, designed to make someone, somewhere, more money, and he was goddamn sick of it. He wasn't sure he could take another day of corporate hell.

He flicked the pen off his desk, and it went sailing across the room, hit the wall and fell to the floor.

"Someday I'll tell you everything," Carson said. "But for now I've gotta go. Thanks for listening to me whine," he said distractedly and hung up the phone.

He continued to stare at the pen, and he knew. Whatever his future held, it wasn't here. It wasn't in this slick, shiny office at Bronson and Wade. And it wasn't in the slick, shiny world of advertising, either. His wild side was calling to him, and he had to follow that voice, wherever it led.

He turned back to his computer, opened up a blank e-mail message, and began typing his resignation letter.

13

LARS DID NOT ENJOY torturing mortals. Rarely did his work call for him to harm one of his own race, and when it did, he hated every moment of it. He was not a cruel man by nature. His work was to protect humanity, not to harm it, and he would have avoided doing so if he could.

But there were occasions such as this, when the mortal world and the supernatural world mixed in an unnatural way, forcing him to lie in wait as he did now. Next to him, Noam was breathing noisily.

"Could you shut the hell up for five minutes? I'm getting damn sick of listening to your nose whistle."

"Screw you," he said in his native Czech. "I've got allergies."

"He should be here any minute now."

"Bastard deserves to die for making it with the witch I want to do."

"We're not going to kill him yet. We're going to get the information we need, and then kill him."

"So what's the plan? You grab him and I inject him with the drug?"

"Yeah. You'd better get the needle ready," Lars said, handing Noam the medical bag they kept behind the driver's seat.

"I've never killed a mortal. Have you?"

Lars nodded. "Once. It's an unfortunate part of the job. You'll come to accept it in time," he said to the younger man, who'd only been his apprentice for six months now.

"What if we capture this guy and he won't talk no matter what? We kill him anyway?"

"Sadly, we'll have no choice."

"Maybe we can use him as bait to lure the witch into our hands."

Lars nodded. "It's possible. That's a last resort, though. Too many uncontrollable variables."

Outside, it had grown completely dark now, which worked to their advantage. They would have to work quickly, and they would have to be ready for any unforeseen circumstance. San Francisco was not the teeming den of witches that L.A. was, but the city had its share.

With any luck, in a matter of days, it would have one less for good.

Noam was glaring out the front window of the van. At nineteen, he was already becoming a decent witch hunter, but he had a lot to learn. Lars could remember himself at that age, twenty years ago, and he remembered his unquenchable idealism, his thirst to free the world of the unnatural balance the witches created.

"My father was killed by a witch," Noam said, and Lars was surprised to hear it. The kid rarely talked about himself. "Killed in the line of duty."

"I'm sorry to hear it. We all have someone we love who was lost to them."

"I swore I'd avenge his life. But if I'm killing another human, that's not exactly vengeance, is it?"

"You have to look at the big picture. This Carson McCullen is one step along the path to eradicating the witches. Don't get bogged down in the details."

"Yeah," the kid said. "I guess you're right."

A movement from the sidewalk up ahead caught Lars's eye. "Hey, that's him," he said, nodding at the man coming toward them. "That's the one we saw on the camera from the witch's apartment."

Noam readied the needle, and the two men exited the van silently. They headed toward the witch's consort, the cool night air enveloping them. Fog was pouring in from the ocean to the west, providing the street and sidewalk with a misty diffusion that aided their plans.

In a matter of seconds, they were upon the man, and he eyed them warily as they parted as if to let him pass between them. But in a lightning-fast movement, Noam had inserted the drug into the man's arm, and Lars caught him as he crumpled to the ground. The two men supported Carson's weight as they walked with his limp body back to the van, and then they dropped his body in the back. The two men climbed in behind him and closed the doors.

A few minutes later, they had him bound with rope in case he gained consciousness before the ride to The Order's Northern California operation center was complete. They were one step closer to capturing Lauren Parish.

A witch foolish enough to go on CNN for her own career glory would be foolish enough to tell them everything they needed to know to take down the entire clan. Lars was sure of it. He'd known, ever since seeing her on the news, that she alone was the key to The Order's success. She was too bold, too proud, not careful like the cowardly elders.

Lauren Parish would be the beginning of the end of the Beauville Clan. But his cock got hard in his pants when he thought of the witch. She was beautiful, even more so than the other female witches he'd seen. She aroused him in a way that he hated. It was impure, unnatural. It was out of balance with nature to desire a witch the way he desired her.

He was not proud of his urge. But as he watched the San Francisco streets pass by while Noam drove, he could think only of taking the witch. He would succumb to his desire if he had half a chance. No harm would come of it, if he was going to kill her anyway.

Surely, one good screw would cure him. And she would hate it, so it would be a form of torture, as well. He could use rape to gain the information he needed.

His erection didn't settle down. Instead, he could

feel his cock leaking seminal fluid in his underpants as he thought of taking the witch. He detested that she could have such an effect on him. He would punish her dearly for that.

"WHAT DO YOU KNOW about Lauren Parish," the man demanded.

Carson blinked at the harsh light, and he felt something warm on his forehead, oozing into his eye. He tried to move his hand to wipe at his eye, but he found that both hands were tied behind his back. He tugged harder, and the rope that bound his wrists cut into his skin.

"Who?" he asked, trying to buy himself a little time.

"Don't play games with me."

Carson could not see the man clearly with the bright light so close to his face. He could only see the dark form of the man on the other side of the light, his face covered by a black ski mask. The man lifted his arm, and then Carson felt the impact of something hard against the side of his head.

He reeled to the side, then was snapped back into place by the ropes that held him in the chair.

"What do you know?"

Carson said nothing. His mind raced to recall his most recent memory before awakening in this chair, in this room, with this man.

He remembered walking along the sidewalk toward his apartment after having gotten off the

Muni after work, his head buzzing with the fact that he'd just resigned from his job. He remembered it being dark, and cold. And then, nothing.

They must have been lying in wait for him. And judging by the throbbing in the back of his arm, like a bee sting, they must have injected him with some kind of drug.

He heard movement from the direction of the man behind the light, and then he felt a stinging slap in the face. Then another. And another.

Carson inhaled sharply at the pain, and he tried to think of whatever tips he'd read in the survival handbook he'd gotten from his brother for Christmas a few years ago. What had the damn thing said about how to survive being tied up and bitch-slapped for information?

Or worse.

The slapping stopped, and Carson had to admit to himself that it was probably the easy part. Something worse had to be coming soon for his enjoyment, or else they wouldn't have needed to tie him up so tightly.

"Let me tell you how this will work," the man said, and Carson noticed for the first time his accent, which sounded Slavic, or maybe German, but he hadn't spent enough time in Europe to know for sure.

"How what will work?"

"You give us the information we need, and we will not kill you."

"And if I don't have the information you need?"

"We kill you."

"You've got the wrong guy," Carson said, pissed at himself for not having read that damn survival guide more closely—for not having memorized it from cover to cover.

"I'm not stupid, Carson McCullen. I know who you are, and I know your relationship to Lauren Parish."

Carson went silent, admitting nothing. He wasn't sure if it would do him any more good to lie and continue denying he even knew Lauren. Or if it was better to play dumb and act as though he didn't know she was a witch.

"Is she worth losing your life over?" the man asked.

Carson concentrated on memorizing everything he could about his captor. The man's gray eye color, the pale skin tone visible through the openings in the ski mask, his wiry build, his black clothes.

"No," he said finally. "She isn't. I barely know her."

And then he remembered something he'd heard about what soldiers were trained to do when captured by enemy troops and questioned. They were told to give only their name, rank and serial number.

Did this occasion count as a capture by enemy troops? Did the rules of war apply here? Were the goals of a U.S. soldier held hostage even remotely similar to his goal in this situation, whatever this situation was?

He didn't want to die, and he didn't want to give away any information about Lauren.

"Do you always screw women you barely

know?" the man said as he sat down at the table across from Carson.

"Occasionally."

Carson thought then of his profession, what he got paid to do for a living in the advertising world. He had to sell a bill of goods to this guy. In short, lie to him. He might not have been a soldier, but he'd been well trained as an ad man.

Which, oddly, probably made him more ruthless than any soldier.

"I should tell you, we know how to kill you and dispose of your body without getting caught," the man said.

"Great. Thanks for letting me know," Carson said wryly, realizing too late that this probably wasn't the time for sarcasm.

And sure enough, the comment earned him another sharp slap. He winced at the stinging that lingered in the side of his face, complemented now by an aching eye.

"These little slaps will start to feel like a welcome respite from what will come after them. Shall I tell you what else will happen?"

"Sure, why not."

"I have a dog," the man said. "He is crazy for the taste of blood. I cut you anywhere, and he will come and attack."

Sounded like loads of fun, though Carson thought it wise to keep the sarcastic comment to himself this time.

"I will ensure the blood is coming from your groin, so he will attack there. If you are unlucky, he will tear your testicles right off. Would you like that?"

Did this guy ever get a yes to that question?

"No thanks. I'd like to pass on that one."

"So then you will cooperate."

Carson nodded, trying his best to look obedient, or however it was a cowed captor was supposed to look.

This was his chance, finally, to prove to himself he really could rise to any challenge. He'd always longed for one of these defining moments, where he could rise above privilege and luck and prove that he was a man to be reckoned with. He wanted to prove he had courage, that he could think on his feet and be counted upon in a crisis.

This was his one chance that would never come to him while working his life away in an advertising firm or whiling away his personal life jumping from one easy relationship to another.

Right here and now, he could not only save Lauren, but he could save his own soul.

"Yes," he lied. "I'll cooperate."

14

LAUREN AWOKE SWEATING, a scream trapped in her throat, her mouth open wide as if she really were crying out for dear life. She inhaled sharply and exhaled, struggling to catch her breath.

The images were too real to have been a dream.

She'd seen Carson tied to a chair, being beaten by a man in a ski mask. She'd felt a grave sense of doom about the situation. And now that she was awake, she understood that it had been a vision.

Not a dream.

Somewhere, Carson had been captured by the witch hunters.

As soon as her mind was free of that vision, another struck her. First the blinding white light, and then an image of Carson stumbling along a road, a cut on his forehead. Over his shoulder, a sign read Hwy 1, Carmel 30 miles.

She rarely had two visions in a row, and she closed her eyes, willing something else to come to her, some other clue to let her know what had happened to Carson, or how she could help.

But nothing else came, of course. She'd been given more than she could have hoped for, except absolute proof he was still alive.

She hadn't protected him, and now he might die. There was a chance they all would, if he talked.

She sat up in bed and blinked at the alarm clock, whose red numbers said it was nearly four-thirty in the morning. Her heart was thudding frantically in her chest. She wiped the sweat from her forehead with her palm.

She had to do something.

God, only five days had passed since Carson had left L.A. How had this happened? How had she let him wander into the hands of the witch hunters? How had she gotten so careless in so many ways? She would not forgive herself, if he was hurt. She wasn't sure how she could go on living with such an awful weight on her conscience.

Lauren got out of bed and dressed, pulled her hair into a ponytail, then went in search of Sebastian. She found him in his office staring at a computer screen, on which there was some spreadsheet that must relate to the nightclub business.

"I need your help," she said before he'd even realized she was there.

He startled, then regarded her calmly. "What is it?"

"The Order has Carson—or had him. We have to find him and help him."

He answered her with a cold, unfeeling stare.

"Sebastian, Carson has a lot of information about us. If they make him talk—"

"We're screwed."

"Exactly."

"Do you see now why I didn't approve of your bringing him here? Humans don't understand the gravity of our situation."

"Spare me the lecture, okay? The damage is done, and we have to try to undo it."

"How do you know what happened?"

"I saw it."

"When?"

"Just now, while I was sleeping."

"You're sure it was a vision and not a dream?"

Lauren nodded.

"You think they caught him in San Francisco?"

"That would be my guess. I saw two visions, one of him being tortured, and another of him stumbling along what looked to be Highway 1, thirty miles from Carmel."

The raven tattoo on Sebastian's arm vanished, and Lauren knew where it had gone—in search of Carson.

"Do I have to tell you what's going to happen if we find the mortal alive?" Sebastian asked.

Of course he didn't. Lauren's stomach lurched, and she cast her eyes down as if she was acknowledging some inevitable sad fact. Though in reality, she'd never let her cousin harm Carson. Not in a million years.

"I'm finished with being patient about him. It's time he pays his dues for entering our world."

"He didn't ask to enter it." Lauren couldn't help pointing the fact out. "It was my fault he came here."

Her cousin nodded. "Have you learned your lesson?"

"Of course."

"And you understand why he has to die?"

Her anger flared, and she didn't dare make herself consider why she was so desperate to keep Carson safe, aside from her sense of personal responsibility to him. "Why not kill me instead? I'm the one who's at fault."

"His death will have a dual purpose—to remind you not to be so reckless, and to keep him from ever endangering us again."

"But if we have the uprising soon, we won't need to worry about him endangering us. The whole world will know who we are."

Sebastian looked at her without expression. "We don't really know when or if the uprising will happen, do we?"

"Corinne seems to think it will happen soon."

"Corinne is young. She has no sense of time."

"She knows more than we do."

"You're not talking me out of taking Carson's life. It's necessary, Lauren. There's no getting around it. I was a fool for letting him be away from us alive for this long."

Lauren's stomach knotted itself tightly. "How can you take someone else's life into your hands so casually? You never used to be that way, cousin."

"I used to be a naive fool," he said flatly.

"You've changed," she said.

"So have you."

Lauren knew the way to Sebastian's heart wasn't this route. She decided to drop the subject for now. "Has the raven found anything yet?"

Sebastian closed his eyes and went completely still for a few moments. When he opened his eyes again, he shook his head. "Not yet."

"I'm going to pack. I think we need to leave for San Francisco as soon as possible. I can go without you if you'd prefer."

"No, I'm going, too. But I have some business to take care of here before we leave. And we should give the raven some time to seek out Carson first."

Lauren nodded, stood and left the office. Her heart was pounding again, and the sickening fear that they might be too late to help Carson clenched her insides. She would try to have another vision, but for now all she had was a sense of doom. Even if they caught up with him and were able to help him escape, she'd still have to save him from Sebastian.

She needed to talk to her little sister because she wasn't positive she could hold off Sebastian on her own. They rarely used cell phones to talk, so she went outside in the early-morning darkness to the pay phone down the block and dialed Corinne's number with a calling card.

After a few rings, her sister answered, sounding as

though she'd been awakened from a dead sleep. "Lauren?" she said in a groggy voice. "Are you okay?"

Without caller ID, she was relying on her intuition to know who was calling.

"Yes, I'm fine. But my friend Carson isn't, and I need your help finding him."

"Carson who?" her sister said, then yawned.

Lauren explained her relationship to the mortal, and then she steeled herself against the humiliation of a lecture from her own little sister. But none came.

Instead, Corinne yawned again and said, "And you're waking me up at *what* time because of this?"

"I'm sorry. I would call another time if I could, but this is an emergency. I need your help now."

"I don't know what you think I can do."

"For one thing, I need you to tell me if you have a sense of what's about to happen. Do you think The Order is close to us?"

Corinne was silent for a few moments, during which time Lauren imagined her sister lying in bed, her long red hair splayed on the pillow and her eyes closed as she tried to summon a sense of the situation.

"I think we still have some time before there is a major clash with The Order, but I don't know how much. Maybe a few years, maybe a year, maybe six months."

"Is that all you're getting?"

"No." And then, a long pause. When she finally spoke again, her voice sounded distant and strange.

"Your vision of you with the man on the beach—it's immediate. It will happen soon."

Lauren blinked, knowing her sister was right.

"If it happens before I see you again," she said, "please remember that I love you."

"I love you, too, Lauren." It wasn't like Corinne to sound vulnerable, but for once, she did.

Lauren couldn't take it. She didn't want to break down and cry. "I have to go," she said and hung up the phone.

Her time had come, whether she was ready or not. She tried not to feel sorry for herself, but she did anyway.

She didn't want to die. She was nowhere near ready to leave this earth. She had way too much living left to do.

SOMETHING WASN'T RIGHT.

Lars had heard the shuffling sound in the rear of the van, but he'd assumed it was simply Carson McCullen stirring in his sleep. The last time he'd checked on McCullen, the man had been knocked out cold, with his hands and feet bound.

But when Lars heard the rear doors of the van open, and caught a fleeting glimpse of McCullen's back as he jumped from the van, he got his first sense that he'd been had.

The bastard was escaping.

But how?

"Stop the van!" he said, lapsing into Czech to

Noam, who was already cursing and pulling over to the side of the road.

Lars scrambled out of the van as it came to a stop, catching the movement of Carson's body as he rolled through the brush and down the hillside. The fool would be lucky if he survived the jump from the van. If he wanted to commit suicide, that was fine by Lars. It would save him having to kill the uncooperative idiot.

As he hurried down the hillside after McCullen, his mind scrambled to understand how he'd escaped in the first place. Perhaps if McCullen hadn't really been unconscious, as he'd seemed to be, and if he'd spent the past three hours in the van working his way loose from his binding, rather than sleeping as Lars had assumed he'd been...

He should have known better than to trust McCullen. He had claimed Lauren Parish was staying at a safe house off of Highway 1, somewhere near Big Sur. He hadn't been very specific with the details, claiming he'd seen the house only once in the dark and couldn't remember much about it, but he would know the place when he saw it.

Lars had knocked him out with a sharp blow to the head, to be safe, tied him up, and they'd set off toward Big Sur, planning to wake McCullen once they were close to their destination.

But now... Now Lars knew he'd been had. He'd never met a human before who'd been willing to die for a witch, so this man had caught him off guard with his stubbornness. Fool had probably gotten so addicted to his witch lover that he could no longer think straight.

Lars tripped on a rock and went tumbling, falling head over heels down the steep hillside, banging himself against brush and rock until he finally came to rest on the beach, his head still spinning. He blinked up at the sky and took inventory of himself. No real damage.

Nearby, he could hear footsteps, probably Noam's, but all other sound was drowned out by the ocean crashing against the beach. Lars sat up and looked around. McCullen was nowhere in sight, but Noam was making his way down the beach, looking left and right.

"Do you see him?" Lars called out as he stood and brushed himself off.

Noam held out his hands and shook his head.

Damn it.

The two men searched until sunset, first the beach, then the woods nearby, and finally they went back to the van and started driving slowly, hoping they'd see something from the road.

In the dark, their task was considerably harder.

Lars stared out at the ocean, at the moon rising over it, and his gut told him they were getting closer to Lauren Parish. Or was that just a foolish, desperate hope, based on how little had gone right today?

"Don't be so pissed off. We'll find him, and we'll find the witch," Noam said, breaking a long brooding silence that had settled between the two men, each probably blaming the other for their escaped prisoner.

"You didn't tie the ropes tightly enough," Lars spat.

"You didn't knock him out like you thought you did," Noam answered, his voice taking on a surly tone.

"You didn't refill the supply of tranquilizers like you should have. If you had, I wouldn't have needed to knock him out."

Lars glared ahead, truly angrier at himself than at the kid, who was young enough to be allowed a few mistakes. Lars knew the source of his mistake. He'd gotten sloppy out of desire. He'd allowed himself to become consumed with thoughts of having the witch, burying his cock inside her, and he had let his usual diligence slide.

He would not forgive himself for that.

Such was the danger of addiction. And he had to remember that he first served The Order. That was his purpose in life, and nothing could stand in the way of it. He believed in his work. He could not let desire interfere.

Never again.

He felt the weight of the gun in its holster against his rib cage, hidden beneath his jacket, and he made himself a promise.

When he found Lauren Parish, he would not let desire overcome him again. He would shoot to kill.

LAUREN SET SEBASTIAN'S BMW on cruise control and glanced at the clock on the dash. It would be dark soon, they had another few hours before they'd reach San Francisco, and she couldn't stop brooding about her own doom.

A witch foretelling his or her own death was not unusual. But Lauren had always hated knowing the circumstances of her own demise. Even knowing that it would probably be the galvanizing action for the uprising didn't help. She didn't want to be a martyr, she wanted to be alive. And now her time was almost up.

She felt twinges of regret about not taking her life more seriously. She would have done a few things differently. She would have loved the people she wanted to love instead of worrying about the rules. She would have let herself live more fully, more honestly…more everything.

Beside her in the passenger seat, Sebastian was sleeping. A sleeping lion, he seemed, likely to awaken and do damage at any moment. The danger he posed to Carson had not escaped her, but she had to trust that, in the end, he wouldn't do anything against her wishes.

The raven was still missing from his arm, still looking for Carson. When it left Sebastian for this long, it exhausted him, put him to sleep. She desperately wanted to know what the bird was seeing now, but it wouldn't do any good to wake her cousin. The raven would return when it had seen what they were looking for.

Outside, the coast stretched on forever north. But

Lauren barely registered the scenery. Her entire being was caught up in the feeling of doom she'd had ever since waking up with the vision of Carson. She couldn't figure out which she felt worse about—that she would soon die, or that Carson might soon be dead himself.

She hated that she'd ever involved him in her life, and she equally hated that once she'd done so, she didn't have the courage to throw out all the rules and let things happen naturally between them.

Maybe they could have proven the elders wrong and had a happy relationship. Maybe Carson could have eventually gotten his fill of her and moved on without any more pain than occurred when a normal romance ended.

Maybe, maybe, maybe. She didn't want to live with such regrets.

If by some miracle she could save herself and Carson, she wanted to give their relationship a real chance.

A movement in the corner of her eye caught her attention, and she glanced down to see the raven tattoo had returned to Sebastian's arm. After a few minutes, he stirred, yawning and stretching. When he opened his eyes, Lauren glanced over at him.

"What did you see?" she asked.

He squinted at the road ahead. "I saw his apartment is empty, so we know he's not there."

"That's not very helpful."

"I wasn't finished. I saw him there on the

highway, just as you predicted. We're only a few miles from his location now."

Lauren's mouth went dry, and she accelerated. When they rounded a bend several minutes later, she could see a man on the side of the road in the distance.

"There he is!" Lauren's heart thudded wildly when, closer, she could see that it was indeed Carson stumbling along the side of the road, the way he had been in her vision.

She pulled the car over behind him.

"This could be a trap, you know," Sebastian said. "I don't think The Order would let him escape without a reason."

"You're right, but we can't leave him here bleeding." She was scrambling out of the car even as she said it.

"Carson!" she called out, and he turned to her.

There was a gash on his forehead, along with dried blood. He looked at her as if she was an apparition.

She hurried to his side. "Are you okay?"

"Lauren, wow. How did you find me?"

"I had a vision of you here with a Highway 1 sign in the background."

"You drove all the way up Highway 1 looking for me?"

"There isn't any time to talk now. I'll explain it all later. Just get in the car with me and let's go."

He spotted Sebastian now in the driver's seat. "I'm not going anywhere with him."

"Don't be stupid, Carson. He's not going to hurt you, but those bastards who did that to you," she said, nodding to his head injury, "will kill us all if they catch up to us."

"What are you talking about?" he said, lifting his hand to his forehead.

He winced when he touched the wound. "What the hell?"

"Do you remember what happened to you?"

He shook his head, frowning as he seemed to try to recall anything. "I remember a room...and a bright light...and being tied to a chair...."

"Nothing else?"

"I don't even remember getting hit on the head."

"It was probably a hard enough impact to make you lose your short-term memory."

"I have no idea how I got here, either."

But Lauren didn't voice her other fear, that whatever had happened to him had been horrific enough to make him block it out.

"We have to go, please," she said again. "Come on."

"You think someone's chasing us?"

"The Order kidnapped you, and I have no idea if they're watching us right now."

He shook his head. "I'm not getting in a car with that guy."

Before she could argue with him any further, the

sound of a twig snapping in the nearby woods caught her attention, and she turned to it. But she saw no one.

"Listen, we have to go *now*. We could all die if we don't hurry."

He seemed to take her seriously then, but a white van screeched around the bend and came careening toward them. Lauren grasped Carson's hand and pulled him in the only direction they could go— toward the beach.

The moon had just risen over the Pacific, providing a little light, but not enough to make it an easy trek down the hillside. She heard a crash, the crunch of metal against metal, and she thought of Sebastian. The sound of screeching tires, and a car engine revving reached her, but she was too far away to guess what was happening.

Soon there was only the sounds of their feet crunching against the dry coastal ground cover, and their ragged breath as they raced toward the beach.

Toward the scene she had been hoping all her life to avoid.

Tears prickled at Lauren's eyes again. This was it. The event she'd been dreading, the place her entire life had been moving toward.

They finally hit the beach, and they made their way across the dry loose sand—too difficult to run fast on—toward the ocean and the wet, hard-packed sand nearest it. Behind them, Lauren could hear someone else scrambling down the hillside.

She said a silent prayer for Sebastian, but she

suspected he would be okay. He, more than anyone else she'd ever met, was invincible, regardless of the changes in him.

Carson was looking to her as they ran, trying to say something. "Where are we going?"

"I don't know, but we need to get off the beach as soon as we can. There's nowhere to hide here."

She regretted now that they hadn't taken the more difficult route into the woods. After all, she'd never had a vision of herself dying in the woods. She needed to get the hell away from this place, this beach with the moon watching over her death.

But when she looked over at Carson again, the moment felt eerily familiar, and she knew it had finally arrived.

15

THE DEAFENING BURST of gunfire at first seemed like a dream to Carson, as if he hadn't really heard it. Maybe his mind was playing tricks on him. Maybe it had been the crashing surf. That had to be it.

He glanced over at Lauren in the instant after he imagined the sound. To his horror he saw her falling forward onto the sand. A dark stain was spreading across her light-colored top, and in his confusion he imagined she must have tripped over a rock, that he just needed to reach down and grab her hand and pull her to her feet again.

His heart was pounding so wildly he could hardly inhale as he bent down, but she wasn't trying to get back up. She was lying facedown on the sand.

Another gunshot. And another.

He dropped to the sand and flattened himself on top of Lauren, stupidly hoping to shield her from the bullets.

When he looked in the direction of the gunshots, he saw two men who'd been pursuing them, both aiming guns in his direction.

But in the blink of an eye, one man fell to the ground, and then the other, watching the first man fall, was struck by some sharp flash of metal and fell, as well.

Carson's mind could not process the events at once. He could think only of Lauren beneath him, of how to keep her safe. He watched the men for a moment longer, but they lay on the ground, not moving. Then he eased himself off Lauren and saw what he did not want to see.

Her back was covered in blood. He could feel the dampness now on his own shirt, and he reached out and touched her back as if to confirm that his eyes weren't fooling him.

He felt as if he were moving in both slow motion and fast forward at the same time, as if the universe was somehow slowing down as it sped up.

This couldn't be happening.

"Lauren," he said, but she didn't stir. "Lauren, please, can you hear me?" he said as he turned her over and found the front of her as bloody as the back.

She'd been shot. Just as she'd said. He would witness her death. He *had* witnessed her death.

But no. He had to save her. Keep her alive.

This couldn't be happening.

He felt her neck for a pulse, but his hands shook wildly, and he couldn't be sure if he was feeling the right spot. He tried to remember what he'd learned of CPR from being a lifeguard in high school, or what he'd learned about first aid before going on his first backpacking trip, but his brain wasn't working.

Finally a coherent thought emerged. He had to stop the bleeding.

He held his hand over the wound, but then thought of how she was bleeding from the back, too, and he started to take off his shirt, when he heard footsteps coming across the sand.

He looked up to see Sebastian running toward them. There was a flutter of black from his arm, and the raven flew to Lauren, hovered over her, and then vanished into her chest.

Carson stared, dumbfounded, unable to process what his eyes had just seen.

Sebastian, breathing heavily, dropped to his knees beside his cousin. His expression was stricken with grief, and tears dampened his cheeks.

"I don't know if that will save her," he said.

"What did you do?"

"I've stopped the wound from bleeding any more, I think. I have to get her to a witch doctor right away."

"We should call 911. We have to get her to a hospital."

"No. I'll take her to a doctor near here. I can't risk anyone asking questions about how she was shot."

"I'll help you carry her to the car," Carson said, knowing by now it did no good to argue with the man. He cared about Lauren almost as much as Carson did, so he had to trust that Sebastian would do right by her.

What other choice did he have?

"First," Sebastian said, looking at him coldly. "Help me dump those bodies into the ocean." He nodded at the men lying on the ground nearby.

Carson looked down at Lauren's face, deathly pale in the moonlight. The rotting scent of sealife in the ocean air made him want to vomit.

This could not be happening.

But it was.

The two men went to the dead bodies, and Sebastian bent and pulled a knife from each of their chests, wiped the blades on his jeans, and inserted them back into leather holsters inside his boots. Carson winced at the sight of the wounds, but said nothing.

He helped Sebastian lift each of the bodies and carry them to the surf, where they heaved them as hard as they could into the cold dark ocean.

"Help me with her now," Sebastian said, and Carson followed along, a zombie helping to carry the limp body of his lover up the hillside.

They lay her in the backseat of Sebastian's car, and the man closed the door and turned to Carson.

"I should kill you now," he said. "I was going to, but you tried to protect her. I can see that."

Carson nodded, saying nothing, his throat constricted at the realization that he had failed miserably. He glanced one more time at her face, too still and too pale and his throat seized up again.

"I loved her," Carson said, much to his own surprise. But once the words had exited his mouth, he understood that they were true.

She wasn't an addiction. It was a feeling of having found the one woman who made him feel whole like no other. She was his cure for a life of numbness. She was his everything.

And now she lay in the back of a car dying. Or, perhaps, already dead.

"Never speak of these events again," Sebastian said. "Do you understand?"

Carson nodded.

"Lauren was right that there are some elements of fate we can't change. Just remember that," he said, and he got in the car and sped away.

Carson watched the car's taillights quickly grow smaller, and then the car rounded a bend in the road and was gone. And here he was alone, at night, somewhere on Highway 1, with a bloodstained shirt, a head wound, and no idea how he'd gotten here.

He looked up at the full moon, at its lonely glow, and knew that this was real. He was here, Lauren was probably dead, and two men's bodies floated in the ocean down below. The gash on his head began to throb as the adrenaline drained from his body, and he reached up and touched it gingerly, trying to guess the extent of the damage.

Hard to tell. He was still up and walking around. But he had no recollection of the hours or days or however long it had been between the time he'd walked toward his apartment after work, and when Lauren had found him limping along the side of the road here.

Other aches and pains began to register, and he was starting to get the picture that whatever had happened to him hadn't been good. It had been, most likely, painful enough that he'd blocked out the memory of it.

Standing at the edge of the road, he looked left, then right. San Francisco was to the north, judging by a sign up ahead that said Carmel was in thirty more miles. So he began walking in that direction.

SEBASTIAN WAS NOT SURE he had made the right decision in letting the mortal live. Hell, the guy looked bashed up enough that he might very well not have made it back to civilization before collapsing dead himself.

But when the moment had come that he should have pressed the blade of his knife into Carson McCullen's neck, he could not make himself do it. He had thought of Maia, of loving someone he couldn't have, and his heart had rebelled at the thought of doing the same thing to Lauren, if by divine grace she somehow survived.

So he left the matter of their fates to chance, and abandoned Carson on the side of the road. Only time would tell if he had done the right thing.

He was a romantic fool.

As he turned into the driveway of the witch doctor's Carmel estate, he blinked back tears. He had never been so scared in his life as he had when he saw Lauren fall to the ground from the gunshot wound. Not even in Bretagne as a little boy, hiding in the woods from the witch hunters.

She had told him over and over that it was her fate to die there on the beach, but he had only realized as he saw it happen how much he had refused to believe it was true.

He still refused to believe it was true.

He had failed his cousin by not saving her, and if by some miracle the part of him wedged inside her chest, attempting to keep her alive, did save her, he would not have to look into her eyes and tell her that he had killed Carson.

So, a fool he was. But he owed her that.

He slammed on his brakes when he reached the end of the driveway, killed the engine, and honked the car horn several times. Then he hurried to the backseat and lifted Lauren into his arms.

He'd already called ahead to their distant cousin Dmitri, to let him know they were on their way and to be ready to tend to Lauren's wound, and as he reached the top of the stone staircase at the entry to the house, the large door opened, and Dmitri stood there already dressed for surgery.

"Bring her downstairs," he said. "Does she have a pulse?"

"I don't think so," Sebastian said, his stomach revolting at the words. "I can't feel one."

At the bottom of the stairs, they reached a room that was brightly lit. Inside, there was an operating table, and a woman Sebastian didn't recognize was preparing instruments for surgery.

He lay Lauren on the table, and Dmitri cut open her top and looked at the wound, his expression grave. "The bullet may have penetrated her heart," he said.

Sebastian felt as if the air had grown thinner, and he needed to sit down.

"Do you think she'll be okay?"

"You should wait outside," Dmitri said. "You don't look well."

"I shape-shifted to stop the bleeding," Sebastian explained. "I'm getting tired from doing so, I guess."

"I will take care of her from here. You return to your full form and go rest for a while."

Sebastian closed his eyes and willed the raven back to his arm. He could feel the strange sensation of slipping from the inside of Lauren's chest, and he could see the dark red of her blood and tissue, and then it was all gone. The tattoo was in its place again.

He glanced at his cousin's pale deathly face as he left the room, and he could not let go of the thought that he had failed her.

Hours later, when Sebastian awoke, drenched in sweat and his heart racing, in a warm room lit by sunlight, he could not say how much time had passed. He did not recognize his surroundings, but the luxury of the linens and the bedroom reminded him that he was at Dmitri's estate, and then the memories of the night before flooded his head.

He had slept fitfully, dreaming awful nightmares

and reliving the events at the beach. He did not know how the surgery had gone, he realized now, and he shot out of bed to find out.

The house was quiet except for a few servants moving about performing their daily chores. Sebastian stopped a maid and asked if she knew where Dmitri was, but she didn't.

He went downstairs to the room where he'd taken Lauren the night before, but the door was locked, and no sound came from within. Muttering a curse, he went back upstairs and wandered around until he found Dmitri in his office.

"What happened?" he said, even though the older man was on the phone.

"I'll call you back," Dmitri said to whomever he was speaking, then hung up the phone and regarded Sebastian. "Good morning. It doesn't look as if you slept well."

Sebastian looked down at himself and saw that he was still in his clothes from the day before. He probably looked like hell.

"What happened?" he asked again. "Is she okay?"

"The bullet passed through her chest cavity and exited from the front. There was damage to her heart. I repaired the tissue as best I could, but please keep in mind I'm not a heart surgeon."

"Is she alive?"

"Her heart stopped beating for a while—I'm not sure how long. We were able to get it beating again, but she's not awake yet. If her brain was deprived of oxygen for very long, she could suffer severe damage."

Sebastian closed his eyes and tried to form a coherent thought. How would he live with himself if he let Lauren die? Damn her stupid vision and her freaking claims that her death was for a good cause. She was too young and vibrant to die.

"When will we know anything?"

"Her body has suffered a major trauma. With some luck, she'll awaken soon and we can tell if she has suffered any permanent damage to her brain."

"And without luck?"

"She may remain in a coma, or she may never be the same again. Or, she may die from the trauma. We should prepare ourselves for any of these eventualities as we hope for the best."

Sebastian took a deep breath. He would have to call her family and tell them the news. But not yet. "I want to see her," he said, and Dmitri nodded.

His cousin led him back downstairs to the room that had been locked. He inserted a key and led Sebastian into the darkened room, where a monitor registered Lauren's vital signs. A slow steady heartbeat blipped across the screen.

The man flicked on a light, and Sebastian saw that a nurse sat at Lauren's bedside, making notes on a clipboard. "Can you give him a few moments alone?" Dmitri said to the woman.

She nodded and left the room.

"Why was the door locked?" Sebastian asked.

"Just as a safeguard. I have to protect myself from the possibility of a police search. If I'm ever caught performing surgeries here, I will be put in jail where I won't be able to help the clan at all."

Sebastian nodded.

"Let Anna know when you're finished visiting, and she'll come back and wait at Lauren's bedside again."

"Is it necessary to have someone with her all the time?"

"With witches who've undergone surgery, it is a wise idea. Our supernatural powers can go haywire when we've suffered a major trauma. It's rare, but I've seen witches accidentally harm themselves while in a coma or while recovering. I'm just covering all the bases."

"Thank you," Sebastian said, and his cousin left the room and closed the door.

He turned to Lauren's body lying on the bed in the middle of the room, and he forced himself to look at her face. She still looked as if she was dead. The color was gone from her features, and her pale skin was a stark contrast to her dark hair.

Sebastian pulled the chair close to her bed, sat and took her long delicate hand in his. It was cool and lifeless.

"Lauren, I hope you can hear me. It's me, Sebastian."

He watched her face for some sign that she'd heard, but there was nothing.

"I did everything I could to save you," he said. "And I'm more sorry than you'll ever know that you got hurt. I know you've got that damn theory about how your death will be the thing that makes Corinne straighten up and learn to control her powers well enough to lead the uprising, but I think you're wrong. I think we need you here, too, if we're ever going to be successful."

He stopped and stared at her hand in his. She'd been his closest friend when they were kids, and he'd always imagined that someday, they'd each have kids who would grow up playing together, being best friends. Tears flooded his eyes at that thought.

He never would have admitted to a soul what a sentimental fool he was, but if anyone knew his true nature, it was probably Lauren. Which made the fact that she was lying here nearly dead hurt even more. If she died, a part of him would die, too.

"Listen Lauren. If there's any way you can pull yourself out of this enough to hear me, you have to do it."

He paused again and squeezed her hand, desperate for something—anything—to get through to her.

"Carson is alive. I let him live for you, you know, so don't ever say I didn't do you a favor. I know you care for him, and you have to get better so you can make sure he doesn't screw everything up for us."

He stopped and watched her face. Still no reaction.

"You see, I'm relying on you to get better so you can keep up with him. You know we can't have some mortal walking around knowing as much about the clan as he knows. If you don't get better, I might have to hunt him down and kill him after all," he said, then immediately regretted it.

Maybe she couldn't take hearing anything stressful right now. But if he knew Lauren at all, he knew she'd get pissed off and fight before she'd give in.

"So get better, so you can watch over that damn mortal. He'd be devastated if you died."

Sebastian kissed her limp hand, then stood and kissed her forehead, too. "Get better, cousin," he said. "Please get better."

LAUREN WAS IN THE MIDDLE of a black place. She felt as if she was suffocating from the blackness. There was nothing to see, nothing to touch, nothing to breathe. A sense of panic rose up in her, and then she realized she could breathe after all.

Her lungs still worked in the blackness. In, out, in, out. She simply had to will them to work, and they did.

But she could see nothing and feel nothing, except for a piercing pain in her chest. It would not go away, instead grew more and more intense.

And then, nothing.

Blackness.

Later, Sebastian's voice. Some part of her watched him talking to her, only half hearing the words. Some part of her sat above them both and felt a heavy sadness that would not go away. She wanted to comfort him, to tell him that all his fighting on her behalf was for nothing and that he should let her go. But she could not.

Later still, more blackness.

And then a fading to brown, to red, to pink, to white. She felt lighter than air, and the pain was gone, or else she simply had entered a place where she could not feel.

She saw herself lying on the bed, and Sebastian was beside her again. He was talking to her, but she heard no words. Her sadness was gone, and she felt only light. She felt as if she had become white light, and she was floating, filling up the space with lightness. There was no longer any part of her connected to that old body, that dying self.

She regarded herself curiously and wondered if she was dead.

Later still came the nightmares, the horrific images of the moments before the bullet had grazed her heart. She saw Carson, with the gash on his head and, she sensed, other injuries not so easily apparent. She saw Sebastian killing the two men who'd been chasing them, and she saw the bodies tossed into the surf. She saw herself, bleeding on the sand, her body lifeless.

She felt as if she was trapped in a nightmare she could not wake from, and she wanted to scream, to pull herself away from the pain and the fear and the sadness. She imagined that she was crying out and thrashing on the bed, and then she could hear her own voice, a dreadful moan. But she didn't know whether she was asking for life or death.

16

THE PROBLEM with giving up his fast-track career, Carson discovered, was that he then had to figure out what the hell to do with himself.

"Catch!" Macy called out, and Carson held up his hand and caught the set of keys careening toward him.

"What're these for?" he asked.

"Can you lock up the office when you're done?"

"Sure, where you going?" he asked as he saved the file he was working on.

"Griffin should be back in a minute, and we've got an off-site meeting with a potential new client."

Macy and Griffin's receptionist had quit a week ago, leaving them screwed until they hired someone new. Carson, suddenly free of a job himself, offered to help them out in the interim.

He hadn't mentioned the fact that he didn't feel like being alone and useless right now, not when he had no idea what had happened to Lauren, and no one to even ask if she was okay.

He'd thought of driving back to L.A. to find Se-bastian and demand to know the truth, but part of him was too afraid to make the trek right now. What if the news wasn't what he wanted to hear? What if she hadn't survived? Part of him had to know the truth, and part of him was too much of a goddamn coward to face it right now.

He'd only started feeling halfway himself again a few days ago. After hitchhiking back to San Francisco thanks to the mercy of a truck driver who hadn't been too put off by his scruffy appearance, a trip to the hospital had confirmed he had a concussion, was in need of sixty stitches, and had suffered various other minor injuries.

He'd been bruised from head to toe, had a fractured rib, and two of his fingernails were missing. The hospital staff had eyed him warily when he swore he couldn't remember what had happened, and they'd forced him to file a police report, but he'd avoided revealing any details about Lauren or her family, or the men who'd been after them.

"What's wrong?" Macy asked.

"Hmm?" he said, jarred out of his thoughts.

"You spaced out there for a minute. You've been doing that a lot lately."

Carson shrugged. "It's nothing."

Macy came back from the doorway and sat on the edge of the desk. "Griffin and I are worried about you. That's the real reason we're letting you work here, because, frankly, you suck as a receptionist."

She smiled at him, but he could barely muster the energy to smile back.

"Are you sure that head injury didn't do any permanent damage?"

Griffin came into the office. "Hey, gang's all here. What's going on?"

"I was just telling Carson that we think he's turning into a nutcase," Macy said.

Griffin smiled. "I thought we weren't supposed to use the word *nutcase* around the n-u-t-c-a-s-e."

"Funny, asshole. I'm fine. I'm just suffering a…you know…broken heart or whatever. Cue the violins now please."

He turned back to the computer monitor and opened a Web browser, intent on looking busy so they'd leave him alone.

"Is that really all it is?" Macy asked. "You weren't probed by aliens or anything while you were gone?"

"That would have been preferable to being dumped, but no, no extraterrestrial probings occurred."

"Damn," Griffin said.

"Don't you two have to be somewhere?" Carson asked, glancing meaningfully at his watch.

"Nah," Griffin said. "I forgot to tell Macy, the meeting's postponed an hour."

"It's about time you fill us in on what really happened with Lauren," Macy said. "She's my best friend, after all. I think I deserve to know what's going on with her."

Carson sighed. He'd been bracing himself for the inquisition, and he knew he couldn't make any more excuses. It was time to make up a really good lie.

"Far as I know," Carson said. "Lauren's fine. She swore me to secrecy about her whereabouts and the reason she had to disappear so quickly from the city, but I can assure you when I left her, she was her usual self."

"I don't get it. Why'd you show up back here looking like you'd had the hell beaten out of you?" Griffin asked.

"I told you, my rental car broke down on the way to Carmel for a little soul-searching getaway. A couple of guys robbed me and kicked my ass when I was trying to hitchhike to the next town."

"Did these guys have, you know, green skin, weird bulbous heads, long probing fingers?"

"Shut the hell up," Carson said, but he couldn't help laughing. It felt good to laugh at something, even if for a moment.

"Did Lauren give you any idea when we'd hear from her again?"

"No, I think she's gotta lie low for a while. But she told me to assure you she really is fine, and she'll be in touch as soon as she can."

Macy was twisting her long blond hair around her finger, and her mouth formed a thin line, but she seemed to accept his answer this time. "If you say so, but if I don't hear from her soon, I'm going to hire a P.I. and start tracking her down myself."

Carson shook his head. "I don't think you want to mess with Lauren. She seemed adamant that we leave her alone for now."

At least he'd gotten through the worst of the withdrawal symptoms since being apart from Lauren. His hands had stopped shaking, he hadn't needed a cigarette in days, and he was down to three cups of coffee in the morning. He even slept on occasion, though not for long, and not without nightmares.

Memories of his time in captivity had started coming back to him. Snapshots of unpleasant and painful moments, torture, his pretending to cooperate with his captors to save himself, only to be tortured even more, and then find that he still had managed to lead Lauren right into their hands.

He would never forgive himself for that.

"There you go again, spacing out," Macy said.

He looked up at her and saw the worried expression on her face.

"Why don't you skip the receptionist gig and come with us to this meeting?" Griffin asked. "We could use your creative expertise."

Carson shook his head. "I'd love to help you out, but my advertising days are done."

Griffin shrugged. "Okay, but the offer stands— you can come work with us any time you change your mind."

"I think I'll stick with playing computer games," Carson said, and navigated to an online game site.

Coloring flashing blocks and mindless Ping-Pong computer games were about the most challenging things he cared to manage at the moment.

"Okay, I guess we'll head on out and beat the traffic," Griffin said, and he and Macy left the building.

Alone, Carson stared at the computer screen without really seeing it. This was the part where he was supposed to be putting his life back together and moving on. This was the part where he was supposed to be relieved to have survived.

But all he felt was miserable. All he felt was that he should have been the one to die.

"Cousin?"

It was Sebastian's voice. Lauren had been hearing it for what seemed like forever, but now she could hear it more clearly. She opened her mouth and croaked a reply.

"Sebastian," she said. Her voice sounded as though her throat had been stuffed with dry leaves.

She opened her eyes and saw a soft overhead light. Next to her, she could hear the beep of some kind of medical machine, and she could hear Sebastian's voice again.

"Lauren, you're going to be fine. I'll get you some water," he said.

She watched him leave the room and come back not with a glass, but with a syringe of water. He put it to her lips and told her to swallow as he gently pressed a little at a time into her mouth.

"The doctor said your throat would be dry, and you'd be hungry, but that you should not take in too much food or drink at once."

Lauren swallowed the water. It felt good against her parched throat.

"What happened?" she said. "Where am I?"

He sat on the edge of the bed and smiled at her. It was rare for Sebastian to smile, and it surprised her, even in her current groggy state.

"We're at cousin Dmitri's house. I'll explain it all soon enough. For now, you should rest."

"Carson," she said. "Where is he? Is he okay?"

Sebastian's smile disappeared, but she sensed none of the hostility she'd come to expect. "He's fine. Don't worry about him."

"Thank you for not hurting him," she said. "He's someone I care very much about."

"I know," he said quietly.

But she didn't think he really knew. Not the full extent of it. She herself hadn't known, until they were on the beach together, and she sensed her life was about to end.

At that moment, all the pretense had fallen away, all the surface crap that didn't matter vanished, and she'd been filled with one solid, unmistakable emotion.

"You were shot in the heart, but it looks like that vision of yours wasn't quite true."

She smiled weakly. "I think I did die," she said. "But I guess I couldn't have known I'd come back to life."

"Thank God you did."

"How long was I dead?"

"Dmitri doesn't know for sure. Apparently it

wasn't long, or else you'd have suffered serious brain damage, according to him."

"Wow," she whispered. "Close call."

"Can you remember anything?"

She nodded, not really ready to talk about it.

He smiled. "Do you feel brain damaged?"

"Not any more than usual."

"I'm supposed to ask the nurse to come in and check you out. I guess she'll ask you some questions and stuff to make sure you're still playing with a full deck."

"Thank you," Lauren said. "I know you saved me, and I know you were with me here the whole time."

He said nothing for a while, and then, "I could not have lived with myself if I'd let you die. I hope you can forgive me for screwing up your vision."

She smiled, but tears filled her eyes. "I forgive you, of course. I didn't want to die."

But she hadn't realized how much she'd wanted to stay alive until she'd felt Carson's body, alive against her, shielding her dying body from the gunfire.

"Your sister's going to be overjoyed to hear from you. We'll call her in a little while, once you're feeling able."

Corinne. She missed her baby sister so much right now. She wanted to see her. "Can she come here?"

"I don't think it would be safe, but we'll get you two together as soon as we can. She was devastated when she heard you'd been shot. I think you were right about that part at least—she might have finally gotten the reality check she needed to understand it's time to stand up to The Order."

"I'm glad I didn't have to die for her to get the message."

"Me, too," Sebastian said, grasping her hand in his. "We all are. How did you know I was with you all this time?"

"I could see you—I could see us both at times. I was sort of watching the whole thing from up above."

"Wow," he whispered. "Maybe you can tell me more later."

"How long was I unconscious?"

"For almost a week."

She wanted to demand he find Carson for her, bring him to her immediately, but she knew that wasn't going to happen. If she cared at all about the mortal, she would stay away from him for good.

"I'd better go get the nurse," Sebastian said, and he left the room.

Lauren tried taking a deep breath, wincing only a little at the pain in her chest. She looked down at her injured body, covered in a crisp white sheet, and she said a silent prayer of thanks that she was alive.

Maybe a near-death experience was what it took to make her understand what mattered in her life. And if so, she was grateful for the bullet that had pierced her chest. Growing within her, she knew, was a will to overcome her injuries, overcome her fears, and overcome anything else that stood in the way of witches never living in fear again.

Lauren would be there to see the uprising. She would be there to help lead it. She would never again live in fear.

17

LAUREN SPENT NEARLY two weeks at Dmitri's house recovering. There was nowhere else for her to go for the time being anyway. But finally, thanks to the witch trait of accelerated powers of healing, she was strong again, and she was restless, and she made preparations to leave. Sebastian wasn't thrilled with the idea, but he'd already mother-henned her half to death.

She wasn't sure yet where she would go, but she knew she had to leave. Standing on the front steps of Dmitri's house, she felt a hand on her arm, and she turned to see Sebastian.

"If you continue, cousin, you're signing up for your own death for real this time," he said.

"What are you talking about?"

"You're not free to wander around anymore. You have to be more careful than ever."

"I'm not going to keep living in fear of The Order."

"It isn't just them. Aunt Leda told me the elders have put a death order on you if you're found consorting with a human again."

Lauren blinked at the news. Her body took a moment to register it, and then she felt the weight of her burden settling in her stomach. Her family was supposed to love her and protect her, not order her death. Or, at least, that's what normal families did. Not for the first time in her life, she wished like hell she hadn't been born a witch.

She jerked her arm out of Sebastian's grasp. "And what? I survived getting shot just so you can carry out my murder like a good little soldier?"

Sebastian leveled his cold gaze at her. "I would never harm you, Lauren. You should know that by now. But you're putting me in a difficult position. My job is to protect witches, and you're making it hard for me to do that when I'm having to expend all my energy on this goddamn mortal boyfriend of yours."

"I'm sorry. I'll get away from you. I can go on from here without your help."

"Lauren, think about this. Is your life worth sacrificing for some mortal?"

"It's not about that anymore. It's about me being able to control my own destiny."

Sebastian sighed. "I'm a supporter of the uprising as much as you are, but there are some rules we have to agree to live by if we want to survive."

"I hate to tell you this, but you're starting to sound like my mother."

"Sorry, but head games aren't going to work with me. Like your mother, I'm worried about you."

"There are some rules I don't agree with, and I'm not going to spend any more of my life trying to avoid breaking the elders' archaic rules."

"There's nothing archaic about not mixing with humans. You're going to dilute the power of the witch clan if you mate with a mortal and produce children."

"Do you know that for a fact?"

"It *is* a fact."

"Which one of us here is the scientist?"

Sebastian glared at her. "What's your point?"

"Genetics don't work that way. One of the greatest threats to the witch clan is inbreeding. The elders' rules are exactly what will do us in as a race, and trying to keep us from mixing with mortals smacks of racism to me."

"We're not exactly a race, you know. It's more than that."

"No, it isn't. Just like with any other ethnic group, our abilities are all in our genetic coding."

"How can our powers not get diluted if we mate with mortals?"

"For one thing, we'll introduce much-needed diversity into our gene pool. Gene pools become increasingly unpredictable as diversity decreases. That's how we manage to have a witch as powerful as Corinne, but it's also how we have fools as useless as our cousin Teal."

"So you think you can reduce the explanation of our supernatural powers to something as simple as genetic coding just like what makes my hair brown or my eyes green?"

"That's exactly what it is."

"That doesn't make any goddamn sense."

"We have no way of knowing for sure since we've had to hide from the lens of modern science."

"So have you been secretly researching this stuff or something?"

In her dreams. Lauren had originally gone into medical research hoping that someday she'd be able to help the world understand witches without persecuting them. But so far, she'd been sidetracked by other projects, like the sexual dumbing-down effect study.

"I've played around a little on my own, studying my own DNA, but I have never done any real research. It's too risky under the current circumstances, and I don't have the support of the elders or the funding that would go along with that support."

"I don't suppose the elders are going to be able to keep us hidden from science forever."

"After the uprising, I think I might dedicate my career to helping mortals understand witches through science."

"It's a noble goal, but you may not even be around for the uprising if you continue with Carson."

Lauren stared out at the cypress trees lining the lawn, and a feeling of intense sadness overcame her. She couldn't see the way forward from here. She'd somehow survived sure death on the beach, and now, her family would kill her unless she stayed away from Carson.

Sebastian wasn't saying it, but they'd likely kill Carson, too.

She couldn't be the cause of his life being threatened again. If she really cared about him, she had to get the hell away from him for good.

A car went by, and she understood what she was facing now. Saying goodbye to everything she loved—San Francisco, her friends, her job, her family…and Carson. She would have to leave it all behind and start a new life somewhere else.

"Promise me something, okay?" she said to Sebastian. "I'm only going to ask you for this one thing, and if you love me, you'll do it."

Sebastian regarded her seriously. "I can't say yes until you tell me what it is."

"Protect Carson after I'm gone. Witch blood does flow through his veins, you know."

Her cousin was silent for a while, and then he nodded. "I'll do what I can."

18

THREE WEEKS HAD PASSED since Carson had watched Lauren get shot on the beach, and he tried to tell himself he was moving on. He was lying.

He'd tried researching new careers on the Internet. He'd gotten a Peace Corps application and filled it out, but he'd never submitted it. And he'd contemplated spending a year at a yoga ashram in India. Nothing quite sounded like the right thing to do.

And then one day he'd been walking along the docks in Sausalito, and he'd spotted a little yacht for sale. He decided on the spot to buy it. He'd had some vague idea he could live in the thing and sail around the world, but mostly he sat on the deck watching the fog roll in, and he brooded.

But today there was no fog. It was one of those perfect crystal blue San Francisco days when the water sparkled like diamonds and sailboats of every color crowded the bay. Carson sat in his usual spot on the deck, feeling as though he should have been doing something. The sunshine did have a vague energizing effect, and the Elmore Leonard novel he'd been reading wasn't quite cutting it for a satisfying activity.

Maybe he'd sail out to the Farallon Islands and watch for whales, or head down the coast, or…

"Hey," a female voice said.

Carson looked up, and his heart nearly stopped at the sight of Lauren standing on the dock.

She smiled. "Can I come aboard?"

He dropped his book on the deck and was off the boat in a split second. "You're okay," he said dumbly as he took her into his arms and pulled her to him.

"I am," she said. "I am."

And then they were kissing. Desperate, hungry kisses that weren't quite satisfying enough, because he needed all of her at once, not just her mouth, not just her tongue. He lifted her up as they kissed, and then he thought of her chest wound.

"Oh shit," he muttered, setting her back down. "Am I hurting you?"

She laughed. "I'm okay—witches heal faster than humans. You can manhandle me as much as you want."

He held her at arm's length and let his gaze linger on her then, taking in every detail. She looked more beautiful than ever, if a bit paler than usual. She wore a black sundress that hugged her torso and exposed her angular shoulders, and tiny black thong sandals that exposed only a small scar on her foot where before a bandage had been.

"I never thought I'd get to see you again. Thank you for coming here, but…is it safe?"

She shook her head. "I can only stay for a little while. I wanted to see you before I left," she said, and something about her voice changed.

Her smile disappeared, and so did his.

"Where are you going?"

"I can't tell you," she said. "But I thought you deserved to know I'm okay, and I owe you a face-to-face apology for all the danger I put you in. I'm so sorry, Carson."

"No, you don't need to apologize."

She said nothing, then eyed the yacht. "Is this yours?"

He nodded. "I was thinking about sailing around the world or something, but I guess I haven't quite mustered the energy yet."

"Macy told me. She sounded worried about you, which is part of the reason I wanted to see you myself."

"Don't worry about me," he said. "I'm fine. Just trying to figure out what to do with myself since I quit my job."

She frowned. "Why did you?"

"I'm done being an advertising whore."

"Good for you. I'm sure you'll find your calling eventually. Just give yourself some time to figure it out."

"Yeah, I guess."

"Want to show me around the boat?"

"Sure, come on board," he said, hopping onto the

deck himself, then extending a hand to help Lauren aboard.

"Down here's the bed," he said, smiling as he motioned to the stairway.

"Oh?" She smiled. "We'd better not go there then."

"Not even once more for old times' sake?"

She shook her head. "I couldn't do that to you again."

"Hey, to be honest, the withdrawal symptoms weren't that bad," he lied.

"I'm glad, but I also have strict orders from my doctor—no sexual intercourse for another few weeks."

"Wow, that's brutal."

She shrugged. "It hasn't been an issue since we've been apart."

"Could I maybe, just, you know, go down on you? One last time?"

Lauren laughed. "You're relentless."

He closed the distance between them and took her into his arms again. Then he kissed her with all the desperate, pent-up passion he felt. When they finally broke the kiss, he asked, "What am I supposed to do with that?"

"I'm sorry," she whispered, but he took her hand and led her below deck and into his bedroom.

She tried to protest as he eased her back onto the bed, but he said, "Please, just this once."

Then he stretched out beside her, careful not to let the weight of his body rest on her torso, and kissed her again, this time more slowly.

He wanted to memorize every inch of her, commit the taste and feel of her to his memory so permanently he would never forget a single detail. Because if she was going to be an addiction that he could never have, then the memory of her would have to be his cure. She smelled like a tropical flower, and her skin was so soft and warm, it reminded him of Caribbean water.

He tugged her dress down and tasted her breasts, then paused to kiss the jagged red scar on her chest. He traced it gently with his fingers and memorized it too. She buried her fingers in his hair and squirmed against him, and he knew when he dipped his fingers into her panties, he'd find her soaking wet.

Then he lowered himself, pulled off her panties, and spread her legs wide, memorizing again her delicious pink folds. When he kissed her there, and inhaled her perfect scent, he almost cried. This was as good as it would ever be, as good as it was going to get.

LAUREN SHOULD HAVE protested, but the truth was that she was as addicted to Carson as he would ever be to her. As he licked her and touched her, bringing her closer and closer to orgasm, she felt her eyes grow damp. She didn't want to say goodbye to him. She wanted to stay here in his bed forever.

He knew how to work her body, and as he touched her in all the right places, she was able, for a little while, to forget. And she gave in to the pleasure one last time. She came hard against his mouth, crying out, gasping, grinding herself against him as the waves of pleasure washed over her.

Then she was still. Catching her breath. He was kissing her belly. Reality intruded again.

"Thank you," she whispered. "I hope you're going to let me return the favor."

"Are you sure your doctor would okay it?"

She smiled at him. "I'm pretty sure he didn't say anything about oral sex."

But he sensed that her mood had changed, and when she tried to sit up, he slid up next to her again and held her in place. "We don't have to say goodbye, you know."

She closed her eyes against their stinging. "Carson, please don't. You know the deal."

"No, I don't. Why don't you fill me in?"

"I mean, you know I'm bad for you, and that people in my world would never accept our relationship. It's just easier if we say goodbye now."

"Where are you going?"

"I've decided it's best if I leave the country and stay hidden for a while. I'm too easy a target—for The Order and other witches. I'll be needed when it's time for the uprising to begin."

"Let me go with you," he said.

"I just told you why that won't work," she said. "Please don't make it harder than it already is."

But some little voice inside her wanted to rebel and told her to hear him out.

"I can leave the country with you. There's nothing keeping me here. I'll help you with the uprising. I don't give a damn what your relatives think, and you shouldn't, either."

"Carson, not only is my life in danger because of The Order, but also the witch clan has a death order on me if I'm caught with a mortal again. They'll kill you, too, if we're found out."

His expression went grim, and he was silent for a while. Lauren felt unwelcome tears building in her eyes. She blinked them away.

Finally, he said, "I have been sitting on this damn boat wondering what the point of my life is, and then you appeared. You, the woman who made me feel what it's like to really be alive."

"I can't put you in any more danger," she said.

"Let me choose that. Please. I think it's my purpose in life now to protect you, to be the human voice for your cause. When your family sees that I can help, they won't want to kill me."

She shook her head, but his words reminded her of the growing feeling she had. The more she thought about the uprising, the more she knew that they would need the help of the mortal world. They just couldn't do it alone.

"We'll go away together until it's time for the uprising to begin. Let me be with you. I don't even have a life here anymore. I might as well be dead if you're not in it."

Suddenly, she was finding it hard to breathe.

"Why would you want to help?"

He looked at her seriously. "Because I love you. Because, when I thought you might be dead, I couldn't find any reason to go on living. I can't think of anything I'd rather be doing than giving us a chance to be together."

Lauren tried to come up with an argument against his words. She was supposed to be protecting him now, not getting him into even more trouble. But…he loved her.

"I love you, too," she said, because she couldn't stop herself.

And she did. Enough to defy the elders' order. Enough to not stand in the way of what he felt was his destiny. Her intuition was screaming that it was the right thing to do.

Then she remembered the vow she'd made to herself when she'd awoken from the coma, that she'd never live in fear again.

He leaned in and kissed her gently again, then said, "Let me go with you. Let me help."

"Okay," she whispered, letting go of the last vestige of fear. "Come with me."

* * * * *

Look for Jamie Sobrato's next
Harlequin Blaze novel!
Coming in October 2007.

THE ROYAL HOUSE OF NIROLI
Always passionate, always proud

The richest royal family in the world—united by
blood and passion, torn apart by deceit and desire

Nestled in the azure blue of the Mediterranean Sea, the
majestic island of Niroli has prospered for centuries.
The Fierezza men have worn the crown with passion
and pride since ancient times. But now, as the king's
health declines, and his two sons have been tragically
killed, the crown is in jeopardy.

The clock is ticking—a new heir must be found
before the king is forced to abdicate. By royal decree
the internationally scattered members of the Fierezza
family are summoned to claim their destiny. But any
person who takes the throne must do so according to
The Rules of the Royal House of Niroli. Soon secrets
and rivalries emerge as the descendents of this ancient
royal line vie for position and power. Only a true
Fierezza can become ruler—a person dedicated to their
country, their people…and their eternal love!

*Each month starting in July 2007,
Harlequin Presents is delighted to bring you
an exciting installment from*
THE ROYAL HOUSE OF NIROLI,
*in which you can follow the epic search
for the true Nirolian king.
Eight heirs, eight romances, eight fantastic stories!*

Here's your chance to enjoy a sneak preview of
the first book delivered to you by royal decree…

FIVE minutes later she was standing immobile in front of the study's window, her original purpose of coming in forgotten, as she stared in shocked horror at the envelope she was holding. Waves of heat followed by icy chill surged through her body. She could hardly see the address now through her blurred vision, but the crest on its left-hand front corner stood out, its *royal* crest, followed by the address: *HRH Prince Marco of Niroli...*

She didn't hear Marco's key in the apartment door, she didn't even hear him calling out her name. Her shock was so great that nothing could penetrate it. It encased her in a kind of bubble, which only concentrated the torment of what she was suffering and branded it on her brain so that it could never be forgotten. It was only finally pierced by the sudden opening of the study door as Marco walked in.

"Welcome home, *Your Highness*. I suppose I ought to curtsy." She waited, praying that he would laugh and tell her that she had got it all wrong, that the envelope she was holding, addressing him as Prince Marco of Niroli, was some silly mistake. But like a tiny candle flame shivering vulnerably in the dark, her hope trembled fearfully. And then the look in Marco's eyes extinguished it as cruelly as a hand placed callously over a dying person's face to stem their last breath.

"Give that to me," he demanded, taking the envelope from her.

"It's too late, Marco," Emily told him brokenly. "I know the truth now...." She dug her teeth in her lower lip to try to force back her own pain.

"You had no right to go through my desk," Marco shot back at her furiously, full of loathing at being caught off-guard and forced into a position in which he was in the wrong, making him determined to find something he could accuse Emily of. "I trusted you...."

Emily could hardly believe what she was hearing. "No, you didn't trust me, Marco, and you didn't trust me because you knew that I couldn't trust you. And you knew that because you're a liar, and liars don't trust people because they know that they themselves cannot be trusted." She not only felt sick, she also felt as though she could hardly breathe. "You are Prince Marco of Niroli.... How could you not tell me who you are and still live with me as intimately as we have lived together?" she demanded brokenly.

"Stop being so ridiculously dramatic," Marco

demanded fiercely. "You are making too much of the situation."

"*Too much?*" Emily almost screamed the words at him. "When were you going to tell me, Marco? Perhaps you just planned to walk away without telling me anything? After all, what do my feelings matter to you?"

"Of course they matter." Marco stopped her sharply. "And it was in part to protect them, and you, that I decided not to inform you when my grandfather first announced that he intended to step down from the throne and hand it on to me."

"To protect me?" Emily nearly choked on her fury. "Hand on the throne? No wonder you told me when you first took me to bed that all you wanted was sex. You *knew* that was the only kind of relationship there could ever be between us! You *knew* that one day you would be Niroli's king. No doubt you are expected to marry a princess. Is she picked out for you already, your *royal* bride?"

* * * * *

Look for
THE FUTURE KING'S PREGNANT MISTRESS
by Penny Jordan in July 2007,
from Harlequin Presents,
available wherever books are sold.

HARLEQUIN®

Mediterranean
NIGHTS™

Experience the glamour and elegance of cruising the
high seas with a new 12-book series....

MEDITERRANEAN NIGHTS

Coming in July 2007...

SCENT OF A WOMAN

by

Joanne Rock

When Danielle Chevalier is invited to an exclusive
conference aboard *Alexandra's Dream,* she knows it
will mean good things for her struggling fragrance
company. But her dreams get a setback when she
meets Adam Burns, a representative from a large
American conglomerate.

Danielle is charmed by the brusque American—
until she finds out he means to compete with her bid
for the opportunity that will save her family business!

www.eHarlequin.com

HM38961

REQUEST YOUR FREE BOOKS!

2 FREE NOVELS PLUS 2 FREE GIFTS!

HARLEQUIN®

Blaze®

Red-hot reads!

YES! Please send me 2 FREE Harlequin® Blaze® novels and my 2 FREE gifts. After receiving them, if I don't wish to receive any more books, I can return the shipping statement marked "cancel." If I don't cancel, I will receive 6 brand-new novels every month and be billed just $3.99 per book in the U.S., or $4.47 per book in Canada, plus 25¢ shipping and handling per book and applicable taxes, if any*. That's a savings of at least 15% off the cover price! I understand that accepting the 2 free books and gifts places me under no obligation to buy anything. I can always return a shipment and cancel at any time. Even if I never buy another book from Harlequin, the two free books and gifts are mine to keep forever.

151 HDN EF3W 351 HDN EF3X

Name	(PLEASE PRINT)
Address	Apt.
City	State/Prov.	Zip/Postal Code

Signature (if under 18, a parent or guardian must sign)

Mail to the **Harlequin Reader Service**®:
IN U.S.A.: P.O. Box 1867, Buffalo, NY 14240-1867
IN CANADA: P.O. Box 609, Fort Erie, Ontario L2A 5X3

Not valid to current Harlequin Blaze subscribers.

Want to try two free books from another line?
Call 1-800-873-8635 or visit www.morefreebooks.com.

* Terms and prices subject to change without notice. NY residents add applicable sales tax. Canadian residents will be charged applicable provincial taxes and GST. This offer is limited to one order per household. All orders subject to approval. Credit or debit balances in a customer's account(s) may be offset by any other outstanding balance owed by or to the customer. Please allow 4 to 6 weeks for delivery.

Your Privacy: Harlequin is committed to protecting your privacy. Our Privacy Policy is available online at www.eHarlequin.com or upon request from the Reader Service. From time to time we make our lists of customers available to reputable firms who may have a product or service of interest to you. If you would prefer we not share your name and address, please check here. ☐

HB07

Romantic
SUSPENSE

**Sparked by Danger,
Fueled by Passion.**

Mission: Impassioned

A brand-new miniseries begins with

My Spy

By *USA TODAY* bestselling author

Marie Ferrarella

She had to trust him with her life....
It was the most daring mission of Joshua Lazlo's
career: rescuing the prime minister of England's
daughter from a gang of cold-blooded kidnappers.
But nothing prepared the shadowy secret agent
for a fiery woman whose touch ignited something
far more dangerous.

My Spy
#1472
Available July 2007 wherever you buy books!

HARLEQUIN®

Blaze™

COMING NEXT MONTH

#333 MEN AT WORK Karen Kendall/Cindi Myers/Colleen Collins
Hot Summer Anthology
When these construction hotties pose for a charity calendar, more than a few pulses go through the roof! Add in Miami's steamy temperatures that beg a man to peel off his shirt and the result? Three sexy stories in one *very* hot collection. Don't miss it!

#334 THE ULTIMATE BITE Crystal Green
Extreme
A year ago he came to her—a vampire in need, seducing her with an incredible bite, an intimate bite…a forgettable bite? Haunted by the sensuality of that night, Kim's been searching for Stephen ever since. Imagine her surprise when she realizes he doesn't even remember her. And his surprise…when he discovers that Kim will do anything to become his Ultimate Bite…

#335 TAKEN Tori Carrington
The Bad Girls Club, Bk. 1
Seline Sanborn is a con artist. And power broker Ryder Blackwell is her handsome mark. An incredible one-night stand has Ryder falling, *hard*. But what will he do when he wakes up to find the angel in his bed gone…along with a chunk of his company's funds?

#336 THE COP Cara Summers
Tall, Dark…and Dangerously Hot! Bk. 2
Off-duty detective Nik Angelis is the first responder at a wedding-turned-murder-scene. The only witness is a fiery redhead who needs his protection—but *wants* his rock-hard body. Nik aims to be professional, but a man can take only so much….

#337 GHOSTS AND ROSES Kelley St. John
The Sexth Sense, Bk. 2
Gage Vicknair has been dreaming—incredible erotic visions—about a mysterious brown-eyed beauty. He's desperate to meet her and turn those dreams into reality. Only, he doesn't expect a ghost, a woman who was murdered, to be able to help him find her. Or that he's going to have to save the woman of his dreams from a similar fate….

#338 SHE DID A BAD, BAD THING Stephanie Bond
Million Dollar Secrets, Bk. 1
Mild-mannered makeup artist Jane Kurtz has always wished she had the nerve to go for things she wants. Like her neighbor Perry Brewer. So when she wins the lottery, she sees her chance—she's going to Vegas for the ultimate bad-girl makeover. Perry won't know what hit him. But he'll know soon. Because Perry's in Vegas, too….

www.eHarlequin.com

HBCNM0607